The Days Run Away Like Wild Horses Over the Hills *(1969)*

Post Office *(1971)*

Mockingbird Wish Me Luck *(1972)*

South of No North *(1973)*

Burning in Water, Drowning in Flame: Selected Poems 1955–1973 *(1974)*

Factotum *(1975)*

Love Is a Dog from Hell: Poems 1974–1977 *(1977)*

Women *(1978)*

You Kissed Lily *(1978)*

Play the piano drunk Like a percussion instrument Until the fingers begin
    to bleed a bit *(1979)*

Shakespeare Never Did This *(1979)*

Dangling in the Tournefortia *(1981)*

Ham on Rye *(1982)*

Bring Me Your Love *(1983)*

Hot Water Music *(1983)*

There's No Business *(1984)*

War All the Time: Poems 1981–1984 *(1984)*

You Get So Alone at Times That It Just Makes Sense *(1986)*

The Movie: "Barfly" *(1987)*

The Roominghouse Madrigals: Early Selected Poems 1946–1966 *(1988)*

Hollywood *(1989)*

Septuagenarian Stew: Stories & Poems *(1990)*

The Last Night of the Earth Poems *(1992)*

Screams from the Balcony: Selected Letters 1960–1970 (Volume 1) *(1993)*

Pulp *(1994)*

Living on Luck: Selected Letters 1960s–1970s (Volume 2) *(1995)*

Betting on the Muse: Poems & Stories *(1996)*

Bone Palace Ballet: New Poems *(1997)*

The Captain Is Out to Lunch and the Sailors Have Taken Over the Ship *(1998)*

Reach for the Sun: Selected Letters 1978–1994 (Volume 3) *(1999)*

What Matters Most Is How Well You Walk Through the Fire: New Poems *(1999)*

Open All Night: New Poems *(2000)*

Beerspit Night and Cursing: The Correspondence of Charles Bukowski &
    Sheri Martinelli *(2001)*

The Night Torn Mad with Footsteps: New Poems *(2001)*

Charles Bukowski

sifting through the madness
for the Word, the line, the way

n e w   p o e m s

edited by john martin

An Imprint of HarperCollins*Publishers*

These poems are part of an archive of unpublished work that Charles Bukowski left to be published after his death.

Grateful acknowledgment is made to John Martin, who edited these poems.

FIRST EDITION

Designed by Cassandra J. Pappas

Jacket art and design by Barbara Martin

Library of Congress Cataloging-in-Publication Data has been applied for.

ISBN 0-06-052735-8

03   04   05   06   07 BG/RRD 10   9   8   7   6   5   4   3   2   1

O3O15 9956

the way to create art is to burn and destroy
ordinary concepts and to substitute them
with new truths that run down from the top of the head
and out from the heart.

contents

part 2

part 3

sifting through the madness

for the Word, the line, the way

part 1

why is it that the pickup truck
carrying the loose refrigerator
on the freeway
is always going between
80 and 90 m.p.h.?

so you want to be a writer?

if it doesn't come bursting out of you
in spite of everything,
don't do it.
unless it comes unasked out of your
heart and your mind and your mouth
and your gut,
don't do it.
if you have to sit for hours
staring at your computer screen
or hunched over your
typewriter
searching for words,
don't do it.
if you're doing it for money or
fame,
don't do it.
if you're doing it because you want
women in your bed,
don't do it.
if you have to sit there and
rewrite it again and again,
don't do it.
if it's hard work just thinking about doing it,
don't do it.
if you're trying to write like somebody
else,
forget about it.

if you have to wait for it to roar out of
you,
then wait patiently.
if it never does roar out of you,
do something else.

if you first have to read it to your wife
or your girlfriend or your boyfriend
or your parents or to anybody at all,
you're not ready.

don't be like so many writers,
don't be like so many thousands of
people who call themselves writers,
don't be dull and boring and
pretentious, don't be consumed with self-
love.
the libraries of the world have
yawned themselves to
sleep
over your kind.
don't add to that.
don't do it.
unless it comes out of
your soul like a rocket,
unless being still would
drive you to madness or
suicide or murder,
don't do it.
unless the sun inside you is
burning your gut,
don't do it.

when it is truly time,
and if you have been chosen,
it will do it by
itself and it will keep on doing it
until you die or it dies in
you.

there is no other way.

and there never was.

.

my secret life

as a child
I suppose
I was not quite
normal.

my happiest times were
when
I was left alone in
the house on a
Saturday.

there was a large
old-fashioned
stand-up
Victrola
in the front
room.
you wound it
up with a
handle on the
right-hand
side.

my favorite time
of the day
was late
afternoon.
it was shady then,
it was
quiet.

I'd take out all the
phonograph records

and spread them
out on the floor
around the
room.

I preferred the
ones with the dark
purple
label.
I only played
those.
but I didn't really like
the
music
very
much.

I'd hold my finger
against the spinning
record
and slow down the
sound.

I liked that
better.

I played all the
records with the
purple label
over and over,
slowing down the
sound.

as I slowed the
music down,
interesting things
happened in my
head
but they were
momentary:
I would see a
waterfall, then it
would quickly
vanish.

or I would see
my father putting
on his leather
slippers in the
morning
or a
tiger killing
something.

I kept seeing
brief glimpses
of many things
before they
vanished
but sometimes
I'd see
nothing unusual,
just the purple
label
revolving
revolving

and I'd attempt to
read the print
as the record
turned.

finally I would put
all the records
carefully
away
and I would
rewind the
machine
and watch the
turntable
spin.
it was covered
with green
felt
and I would
alter the speed
of the turntable
by holding my
finger against
it.

after that,
I would go to
the front window
and peek through the
drapes at the lady
across the street.
she sat on the
front steps

of her house
most of the day,
her legs crossed
as she smoked
her cigarettes.
she spoke to our
neighbors as they
walked by and
she had long silken
legs.
she laughed often
and seemed
happy:
she was not
at all
like my
mother.

I'd watch her for
a long
time.
I'd watch her
until she went
back into her
house.

next was the
clock on the
mantel.
it had a large
sweeping
second
hand.

then the contest
would
begin:
me against the
second
hand.

I would position
myself on the
floor
so that I could
watch
the second
hand.

I would wait until
it touched the
twelve,
then I would
hold my
breath.
I would hold
it as long as
possible,
timing
myself.

then I would
begin
again,
holding my
breath
in an attempt

to hold it
longer than
I was able to
the last
time.

I would note the
time that had passed,
then I would
begin once again
in an
attempt to
better that
time.

each time
I would
be able to hold
my breath
a little
longer.

but it became
more and more
difficult.

I'd hear an
excited announcer's
voice:
"THIS TIME, LADIES
AND GENTLEMEN,
THERE WILL SURELY BE A

NEW WORLD'S
RECORD!"

it got hard,
it got very hard,
holding my breath,
but the world
record was
important.

I could no longer
just lie there
holding it
in,
I had to clench
my fists
and roll about on
the rug.
I'd close my eyes
while
flashes of light
exploded inside
my head,
explosions of color,
red, blue,
purple!

at last,
I'd breathe
in and
look at the
clock:

I HAD SET A NEW
WORLD'S RECORD
15 SECONDS LONGER
THAN THE OLD
ONE!

then I'd get
up,
go into the
kitchen and drink
a glass of
water.
I always drank a
glass of water,
then.
I don't know
why.

soon after that
my parents would
come home,
first my mother,
then my
father.

my mother wouldn't
say much,
she'd be busy in
the kitchen,
but my father
always had something
to say
and it was always

the
same:
"well, Henry, what
have you been doing
all day?"

"nothing."

"nothing? what the
hell kind of answer is
that?"

I wouldn't reply,
not to him,
he would never
know,
I'd die before I
would tell him
anything,
he could kill me
before I'd tell
him.

him and his shoes,
him and his ears,
him and his hairy
arms.

whatever it was
I had
done,
it belonged only to
me.

the column

to avoid the inexplicable had always been
a necessity for me.

and so this day in 1942
I was 21 years old
sitting on a park bench
with and like the
other bums

when the war chariots
rolled by

soldiers on their way
to war
and the soldiers saw
me
hated me

began yelling and cursing
at me

asking me what the hell I
thought I was doing there!

I was the only young bum
in the park.

the soldiers wanted me to be going
with them.

the whole column of them
screamed and cursed at
me

as they drove
by.

then the column was
gone and the old bum
next to me
asked, "how come you
ain't in the Service,
son?"

I got up and walked
down to the library.

I went inside
found a book and
sat down
at a table.

I began to read
the book.
the meaning was
too deep
for me
then.

so I put it
back on the shelf
walked back outside
and waited.

commerce

I used to drive those trucks so hard
and for so long that
my right foot would
go dead from pushing down on the
accelerator.
delivery after delivery,
14 hours at a time
for $1.10 per hour
under the table,
up one-way alleys in the worst parts of
town.
at midnight or at high noon,
racing between tall buildings
always with the stink of something
dying or about to die
in the freight elevator
at your destination,
a self-operated elevator,
opening into a large bright room,
uncomfortably so
under unshielded lights
over the heads of many women
each bent mute over a machine,
crucified alive
on piecework,
to hand the package then
to a fat son of a bitch in red
suspenders.
he signs, ripping through the cheap
paper
with his ballpoint pen,
that's power,
that's America at work.

you think of killing him
on the spot
but discard that thought and
leave,
down into the urine-stinking
elevator,
they have you crucified too,
America at work,
where they rip out your intestines
and your brain and your
will and your spirit.
they suck you dry, then throw
you away.
the capitalist system.
the work ethic.
the profit motive.
the memory of your father's words,
"work hard and you'll be
appreciated."
of course, only if you make
much more for them than they pay
you.

out of the alley and into the
sunlight again,
into heavy traffic,
planning the route to your next stop,
the best way, the time-
saver,
you knowing none of the tricks
and to actually think about
all the deliveries that still lie ahead
would lead to

madness.
it's one at a time,
easing in and out of traffic
between other work-driven drivers
also with no concept of danger,
reality, flow or
compassion.
you can feel the despair
escaping from their
machines,
their lives as hopeless and
as numbed as
yours.

you break through the cluster
of them
on your way to the next
stop,
driving through teeming downtown
Los Angeles in 1952,
stinking and hungover,
no time for lunch,
no time for coffee,
you're on route #10,
a new man,
give the new man the
ball-busting route,
see if he can swallow the
whale.

you look down and the
needle is on
red.

almost no gas left.
too fucking bad.
you gun it,
lighting a crushed cigarette with
one hand from a soiled pack of
matches.

shit on the world.

the Mexican fighters

watching the boxing matches from Mexico
on tv while sitting in bed
on a cool November evening.
had a great day at the track, picking 7
of 9, two of them long shots.
no matter, I am watching the fighters
work hard now, showing more courage than
style
as in the front row two fat men talk to
each other,
paying no attention to the
boxers
who are fighting for their very existence
as human beings.
sitting in bed here, I feel sad for
everybody, for all the struggling people
everywhere, trying to get the rent paid on time,
trying to get enough food, trying to get
an easy night's sleep.
it's all very wearing and it doesn't stop until you
die.
what a circus, what a show, what a
farce
from the Roman Empire to the French-
Indian War, and from there to here!

now, one of the Mexican boys has
floored the other.
the crowd is screaming.
the boy is up at 9.
he nods to the referee that he is
ready to go again.
the fighters rush together.

even the fat men in the front row are
excited now.
the red gloves fiercely punch the air and the
faces and the hard brown
bodies.

then
the boy is down again.
he is flat on his back.
it's over.

the god-damned thing is over.

for that boy, there is no knowing where he is
going now.
for the other boy, it's going to be good for
a little while.
he smiles in tune with the
world.

I flick off the tv.

after a moment I hear gunshots off somewhere in the
distance.
the contest of life continues.

I get up, walk to the window.
I feel disturbed, I mean about
people and things, the way of
things.

then I'm sitting back on the bed, with many
feelings passing through me that I can't quite

comprehend.

then I force myself to stop thinking.
some questions don't have answers.

what the hell, I had 7 for 9 at the track today, that's something
even in the midst of a lot of
nothing.

what you do is take whatever luck comes your way and pretend
you know more than you ever
will.

right?

this dog

look at this place! stockings and shorts and trash all
over the floor! you just don't want to be responsible!
to you a woman is nothing but something
for your *convenience!* you just sit there slurping up
everything I do for you!
why don't you say something?

this is your place so you have to listen! if I was
talking to you like this at my place you'd walk right
out the door!

why are you smiling?
is something funny?

all you do is slurp up all my love and caring
and then go to the racetrack!
what's so great about a horse?
what's a horse got that I haven't got?

four legs?

aren't you bright?
aren't you funny?
now aren't you the thing?

you act like nothing matters!
well, let me tell you something, asshole, *I matter!*
you think you're the only man in this town?
well, let me tell you, there are plenty of men who
want me, my body, my mind, my spirit!

many people have asked me, "what are you doing
with a person like him?"

what?
no, I don't want a drink!
I want you to realize what's happening to our relationship
before it's too late!

look at you still slurping all this up!
you think you're so wonderful!
you know what happens to you when you drink
too much?
I might as well be living with a eunuch!

my mother warned me!
everybody warned me!

look at you now!
why don't you try to communicate?
why don't you shave?
you've spilled wine all over the front of your shirt!
and that cheap cigar!
you know what that thing smells
like?
like horseshit!

hey, where are you going?
to some bar, to some stinking bar!
you'll sit there nursing your self-pity
with all those other losers!

if you go out through that door I'm going
out dancing!
I'll go meet a new man!
I'll go have some fun!

if you go out that door, then it's over between us forever!

all right, go on then, you asshole!

asshole!

asshole!

ASSHOLE!

the great escape

listen, he said, you ever seen a bunch of crabs in a
bucket?
no, I told him.
well, what happens is that now and then one crab
will climb up on top of the others
and begin to climb toward the top of the bucket,
then, just as he's about to escape
another crab grabs him and pulls him back
down.
really? I asked.
really, he said, and this job is just like that, none
of the others want anybody to get out of
here. that's just the way it is
in the postal service!
I believe you, I said.

just then the supervisor walked up and said,
you fellows were talking.
there is no talking allowed on this
job.

I had been there eleven and one-half
years.

I got up off my stool and climbed right up the
supervisor
and then I reached up and pulled myself right
out of there.

it was so easy it was unbelievable.
but none of the others followed me.

and after that, whenever I had crab legs
I thought about that place.
I must have thought about that place
maybe 5 or 6 times

before I switched to lobster.

a quick one

in 5 minutes I am going
to get into my
jacuzzi
but first please take
a picture of this:
a 70-year-old
white whale lurking
within the warm white
whirling water.

how did he last?
how did he escape
all the harpoons
for all those years?
why didn't he get beached
along the way
on the dry
shore?
how did he evade so many
schools of hungry
sharks?

now see this:
his little eyes peering just
above the bubbling
water . . .

what a miracle!

life is full of happy
miracles
here in the cool dark
winter evening.

in the stratosphere
the jealous gods shiver
and moan
while
the white whale floats
blissfully
in the warm white
water
where it's always
104 degrees
of
heaven on
earth.

the old anarchist

my neighbor gives me the key to his house
when he goes on vacation.

I feed his cats
water his flowers and his
lawn.

I place his mail in a neat stack
on his dining room table.

am I the same man who planned to
blow up the city of Los Angeles
15 years ago?

I lock his door.
I walk down his front walk
pause
stretch a moment
in the sunset thinking,
there's still time,
there's still time for a
comeback.
I have never belonged with
these others.

I walk down the sidewalk
toward my place

being careful
not to step
on the cracks.

and I still won't vote

10 boxes of crackerjack left over from
Halloween.
I give them to the gardeners.

I am the great man on this plantation.
I bring beer to the workers.

they play their transistor radios
listen to the crap music
in the sun.
they suck at their beer,
break open the boxes of
Crackerjack.

they chew
rotting their mouths and their brains
as I phone my financial adviser at
Salomon Brothers.

he says, copper, put it into
copper.

I'll consider that, I tell him.

I hang up, walk out on the
balcony, watch the men in the 98-degree
heat.

"you're doing a great job, fellows!"

a nice bright-eyed fellow up near the
front
asks,

"do you want us to do the planting too?"

"no, you fellows do the shit work, I'll
do the planting, I'll take the glory."

they don't laugh.
I wave, walk back inside.

then I feel the need to excrete.
I ponder whether to use
the front crapper
the back crapper
or
the upstairs crapper.

I decide on the upstairs crapper, walk
up the marble stairway thinking, it has
taken you sixty years, Chinaski, to finally
plunder the American economic system.

just trying to do a good deed

she was right when she told me, "you
only go with my sister because she's
younger than I am. you're prejudiced
against older people and dislike fat
women."

"when's she coming home?" I asked
her. "where is she?"

"don't worry about her, I'm talking to
you now.
tell me, what's wrong with me?"

"you're too old and you're fat," I told
her.

"but so are you," she said.

"I'm not fat," I said.

"you're overweight," she said.

"all right, stop bitching, come on,
we'll fuck."

"what did you say?"

"you heard me."

we sat there without speaking then.
I nodded toward the bedroom a
few times but she just sat
there.

suddenly the door opened and the
younger sister appeared.
the fat sister jumped up.

she pointed to me.

"HE WANTED TO FUCK ME!"

the younger sister looked at me.

"is this true?"

"no," I said, "I didn't want to."

"BUT HE OFFERED TO!" screamed the
older sister.

"well?" the younger sister asked me.

"it's true," I said.

"YOU GET OUT OF MY HOUSE!"

I got up and walked out the door
and across the sidewalk to my
car.

"I TOLD YOU HE WAS NO GOOD!"
I heard the fat sister scream.

"OH, SHUT UP!" I heard the younger
sister scream.

I got into my car and drove
away.

when I got to my place the phone
was ringing.
I picked it up, hung it up,
then took it off the
hook.
better to be safe than
sorry.

one step removed

I knew a lady who once lived with Hemingway.
I knew a lady who claimed to have screwed Ezra Pound.
Sartre invited me to visit him in Paris but I was too stupid to
accept.
Caresse Crosby of Black Sun Press wrote me from Italy.
Henry Miller's son wrote that I was a better writer than his
father.
I drank wine with John Fante.
but none of this matters at all except in a romantic sort of
way.
some day they'll be talking about me:
"Chinaski wrote me a letter."
"I saw Chinaski at the racetrack."
"I watched Chinaski wash his car."
all absolute nonsense.
meanwhile, some wild-eyed young man
alone and unknown in a room
will be writing things that will make you forget
everybody else
except maybe the young man to
follow after
him.

my life as a sitcom

stepped into the wrong end of the jacuzzi and twisted my
right leg which was bad to begin with, then that night got drunk
with a tv writer and an actor, something about using my
life to make a sitcom and luckily that fell through and the next
day at the track I get a box seat in the dining area, get a
menu and a glass of water, my leg is really paining me, I
can barely walk to the betting window and back, then
about the 3rd race the waiter rushes by, asks, "can I
borrow your menu?" but he doesn't wait for an answer,
he just grabs it and runs off.
a couple of races go by, I fight through my pain and continue to
make my bets, get back, sit down just as the waiter rushes by again.
he grabs all my silverware and my napkin and runs off.
"HEY!" I yell but he's gone.
all around me people are eating, drinking and laughing.
I check my watch after the 6th race and it is 4:30 p.m.
I haven't been served yet and I'm 72 years old with
a hangover and a leg from hell.
I pull myself to my feet by the edge of the table and manage
to hobble about looking for the *maitre d'*. I see him down
a far aisle and wave him in.
"can I speak to you?" I ask.
"certainly, sir!"
"look, it's the 7th race, they took my menu and my silver-
ware and I haven't been served yet."
"we'll take care of it right away, sir!"
well, the 7th race went, the 8th race went, and
still no service.
I purchase my ticket for the 9th race and take the
escalator down.
on the first floor, I purchase a sandwich.
I eat it going down another escalator to the parking lot.
the valet laughs as I slowly work my leg into the

car, making a face of pain as I do so.
"got a gimpy leg there, huh, Hank?" he asks.
I pull out, make it to the boulevard and onto the
freeway which immediately begins to slow down because
of a 3-car crash ahead.

I snap on the radio in time to find that my horse
has run out in the 9th.
a flash of pain shoots up my right leg.
I decide to tell my wife about my
misfortunes at the track
even though I know she will respond
by telling me that everything as always
was completely my fault
but when a man is in pain he can't think right,
he only asks for
more.

and
gets it.

a mechanical Lazarus

I don't know how long I've had this
IBM Selectric typewriter: 12 years
maybe: it's typed thousands of poems,
dozens of short stories, two or three
novels and a screenplay.

I've spilled beer, wine,
whiskey, vodka, ale plus
cigarette and cigar ash
into it
with never a breakdown.

and I don't know how many hours
of classical music we've listened
to together.

the nights have always been
long and good
with always the promise of
laughter behind our most
serious
moments.

then I received a computer for
Christmas.

I mean, we must keep up with the
times. no?

after all, the old manual standard
that preceded the electric typewriter
now sits downstairs
in dignified retirement

and we too have shared many
magical and crazy
nights.

I mean, men once wrote with
quill pens.
we must move on.

so I cleared the desk off for the new
computer.

then I pulled the plug on the
electric, covered it and
carried it over to the corner
of the room and set it
down.

that was the worst part—carrying it off
like that.

it was like it was something alive.

I half expected it to speak,
as it often had, in its own
way.

I felt as if I had turned a pet
dog out into the cold
street.

then my daughter
who is a computer whiz
came over to set things up

for me and to show me
the basic techniques.

she left and I began playing
with the computer.
it did some wonderful
things
but then I noticed certain
inconsistencies.
the machine wouldn't do
some of the things they claimed
it would.

my wife tried her hand at
it.
same thing.

so we shut the machine down
and went to
sleep.

the next day
when I came home from the
track
my wife told me that the
computer had a glitch or a
possible
virus.
my daughter had worked on it
all afternoon to
no avail.

so
for the time
being
my old IBM has
risen from the grave,
the bottle of beer
is to my left, and the little red
radio to my right is
playing
Bach.

my old
electric warrior
is back
typing this now
as the many parts of the
computer are
scattered across the
rug.

bravo!

my god

you know that little girl
who used to play
on the lawn across the street?

look what happened
overnight:

new breasts
round ass
long legs
long hair

eyes of
blue fire.

we can no longer
think of her
as before.

now she is
15 years full of
trouble.

after the sandstorm

coming off that park bench after the all-night
sandstorm in El Paso
and walking into the library
I felt fairly comfortable even though I had less than
two dollars
was alone in the world
and was 40 pounds underweight.
still it felt almost pleasant to
open that copy of the *Kenyon Review* in
1940
and marvel at the brilliant way those
professors used the language to take one another
to task for the way each interpreted literature.
I almost appreciated their humor and sarcasm,
but not quite: the professorial envy for one another
was a bit too rancid and
red-steel-hot; but at the same time I envied the
leisurely and safe lives that language and literature
had evolved for them: places safe and
soft and institutionalized.
I knew that I would never be able to write or live in
quite that manner, yet I almost wanted to be
one of them then,
at that moment.

I put the magazine back and walked outside,
looked south north east west

each direction was wrong.
I started to walk along.

what I did sense was that language
properly used

could be bright and beautiful but
I also sensed that there might be
some more important things I had
to learn
first.

carry on!

the famous actor came by, I poured him a wine
as he sat near the warm fireplace. he was
really a nice fellow, had been in the business
for decades, said that he really liked what I
wrote. I told him, "thank you," and poured him
another wine.

then he began to describe his new tv
series about a man and a woman
who adopted 3rd World children that nobody else
wanted.

"I mean," he said, "we're going to try to capture
the spirit of
loving family relationships and the goodness of
it all."

he was quite sincere, nothing phony about his
desire.

"I realize," I said, "that uplifting family
programs are becoming very
popular but . . ."

(I was thinking of the black actor, also with
great talent,
who was on top of the ratings with his
black family
but I often wondered what blacks in
the ghettos thought about the comfortable
problems of those well-dressed, well-fed
actors)

". . . but there is another kind of family series
I'd like to see that's more real and
more a part of our culture."

he smiled. "what's
that?"

"I'd like to see a series about a guy who works
all day long in a factory, fighting to keep the job
he hates but is afraid of losing, while the foreman continually
chews out his ass during the long hard hours.
this guy finally punches out at the end of the day,
gets into his old car and is grateful when it starts just one more
        time.
then he drives back to his flat where the rent
eats up one-half of his salary. he walks
in the door where his 3 kids in filthy clothes and
dirty faces are bouncing a tennis
ball against the walls while his fat wife is
passed out on the couch, snoring.
then he walks into the kitchen and the family
dinner is burnt black on the stove with the
gas still turned up high."

"well," said the actor, "what *we* are trying
to do is uplift the spirit of the people, give
them hope and some sense of what a loving family
is like."

"yes," I agreed, "that's nice
too."

we talked some more and I mentioned

some of the movies I had seen him in and
enjoyed.

he kindly countered, singled out some of my
writing that had pleased him.
then he had to leave, told me, "listen, we
have to get together soon again!"

"anytime," I
said.

he phoned a couple of days later early in the
morning
and read me a poem about a fantasy baseball game:
if you had 2 strikes against you: "CARRY ON!"
and if you dropped an easy fly ball:
"CARRY ON!" and if you were one run behind in
the 9th inning with 2 outs and you struck out with
the bases loaded: "CARRY ON!" and etc.

and
it was a rhyming
poem.

"thank you very much," I told
him.

"we've just got to get together again,"
he said. "I love the way you talk!"

"sure," I said, "anytime you get the
chance. my time is
anytime."

I waited a few days, then phoned him
twice.
once I got somebody who was
a secretary of some
sort.
the next time I got his
wife.

each time I left the message that
I was looking forward
to a visit from the famous
actor.

but now
weeks have gone by and still no
word.

well, a family tv series can be a
very demanding
experience.
people get busy, you know
that.

the other night I was sitting in front
of the cable
flicking the remote control
and there came *his* face on the
screen
in some old
movie.

I watched: a tremendous talent, no
doubt.

then I hit the remote control again and got the
wrestling matches: Greenbutt Gus vs.
The Swamp Man.

both also
tremendous
talents,
no doubt.

straw hats

I would never buy one, not at my
age, and I was never a
hat man anyhow
but then
that's what wives are for:
to give you the incentive to
dive into uncharted
waters.

"go on, go on in," said my
wife.

so I went into the shop and she
followed.
there were straw hats
everywhere, all colors and
sizes.

I tried on a black one, walked to
the mirror, looked like a killer
and, of course, liked that one best
but
returned the hat
anyhow.

"here," said my wife,
"try this."

I tried it on. not
bad. then
another one. not
bad.

I decided on those two.
holy hell!

I liked the clerks, they were
totally
uninterested.

"should I put them in a
bag?" one of the clerks
asked.

"a box," I replied.

then
my wife came around the corner,
smiling, wearing a
straw hat
with a very wide brim.
she looked much better than
I.
she looked
cute.
beautiful.

"get it," I
said.

"should I?"

"of course."

so we walked out of there with
our new straw

hats
and we took them back
to the car
and put them
in their boxes
on the back
seat
and it was a good drive
home
under the low
clouds,
nothing wrong at
all.
very strange and
totally
acceptable.

and I never would have
worn the black one
anyhow.

drink and wait

well, first Mae West died
and then George Raft,
and Eddie G. Robinson's
been gone
a long time,
and Bogart and Gable
and Grable,
and Laurel and
Hardy
and the Marx Brothers,
all those Saturday
afternoons
at the movies
as a boy
are gone now
and I look
around this room
and it looks back at me
and out through
the window pane,
time hangs helpless
from the doorknob
as a gold
paperweight
of an owl
looks up at me
(an old man now)
who must endure
these many empty
Saturday
afternoons.

basking in the evil light

it all happened
many years ago
at Eveningtide Jr. High School.
I suppose it started in the boys' shower
after gym class when we decided
that Harold Flemming had the
largest penis at
Eveningtide, only
in Harold's case his penis was,
we decided,
almost beyond
human comprehension.

anyhow, he had a big
one and
the word got
out
and almost everybody knew about
it except
Miss Tully who taught
Biology.

the boys knew, the girls knew, the
gym teachers
knew
and
for some reason
it really bothered Masterson who
taught gym.
he was a little bully with a pot
belly who had the
hots for

Mrs. Gredis who taught
English.

well, there were 3 of us who
hung out
together:
me, Danny Hightower and Harold
Flemming.
Masterson kept giving us
hard looks for no
reason.

one day he stopped us
outside the
cafeteria: "I'm going to
find out what you 3 are
up to even if I have to
follow you to the
ends of the
earth!"

we laughed at him because
we hadn't done
anything wrong.

when we laughed he got
pissed and gave us
2 weeks on
lunch-garbage
detail.

on that detail we emptied
garbage cans

during lunchtime
and speared
pieces of paper with
nail-tipped sticks.

the girls watched us
and
giggled while
slyly glancing at Harold
Flemming.
they also
put their heads together and
whispered while they
giggled.

it felt great to get all
that
attention.
Danny Hightower loved
it too.
Flemming?
well, he never said
much.

then it happened over-
night: one day I came to
school and both Danny Hightower and
Flemming were
missing.

I soon got the
word: Harold
Flemming had

had intercourse with some
girl
behind the
chemistry building and
had
almost
torn her
apart.

and somehow Danny
Hightower was
involved.
but what he had
to do with it
wasn't entirely
clear.

then
a couple of
weeks later
further word
came down: Harold
Flemming and Danny
Hightower were at
Gateford Hills, the Boys
Reformatory.

it was soon after
that when
Masterson
stopped me outside the
cafeteria.

he looked very
intense.
he looked like he was
ready to
swing at me.

I hoped he
would.
I felt I could take
him.

"all right," he said,
"I know you were there!
I'm going to
get you
too!"

"yeah?" I
asked.

"you think I
won't?"

I didn't
answer.

"stop *sneering!*" he
yelled.

I hadn't
realized
that I
was.

"2 weeks garbage!" he
yelled.

I shrugged and walked
off
pretending to be
very tough and
evil
pretending I was
just one more
great secret fucker of
jr. high school
girls

but I knew
without Harold Flemming
at my side
that I was
nothing

and worse

the girls knew it
too.

what can I do?

it's true:
pain and suffering
helps to create
what we call
art.

given the choice
I'd never choose
this damned
pain
and suffering
for myself
but somehow it finds
me

as the royalties
continue to
roll on
in.

out of the sickroom and into the white blazing sun

hey, you're not dead, you're
doing good, damned good again,
what's this talk about tossing it
in?

what you were doing while you
were feeling sick enough
to die,
what you were really doing was just re-
charging your
batteries.

now let everybody get
out of the way,
you're thundering
down the track again
like a locomotive
hauling 90 thousand
unwritten poems
and they're all
yours
and you're pounding along
the rails
sometimes through dark tunnels
but then roaring out again
into the
light!

who the hell said that
you no longer had it in
you?

it was you who said that.

the engineer

who is now
feeling a fresh surge of
hope and
power
and who is
grinning madly at the
thought of this
wonderful
new
day.

temporal ease

you can't know how good it feels driving in for a wash-
and-wax with nothing to do but light a cigarette and
wait in the sun with no overdue rent, no troubles to speak of
as you hide from the whores.

now here it comes, clean, glistening black, you tip the man
$2, get in, run up the aerial, adjust the side mirror,
start the engine, turn on the radio classical, move out
into the street.

open the sun roof, take the slow lane, hangover gone,
you're sleepy in the sun . . . and then you're there.

the parking lot attendants know you: "hey, Champ,
how's it going?"

inside, you open the *Racing Form*, decide to spend the day
with the runners . . . already you've spotted two low-
price sucker bets in the first race that will not
win—that's all you need, an edge.

"Hank . . ."

it's somebody behind you, you turn, it's your old
post office buddy, Spencer Bishop.

"hey, Spence . . ."

"hey, man, I hear you been fooling the people, I
hear you been going around to the universities and
giving lectures . . ."

"that's right, my man."

"what are you going to do when they find you out?"

"I'll come back and join you."

you go to your seat and watch them come out for the
post parade
(you could be painting or in the botanical gardens)
but the 6 looks good in the *Form* and in the flesh.
½ is not the world but it's over a third.

you get up and move to the windows.
the screenplay is finished, you're into the 4th
novel, the poems keep arriving, not much going on with
the short story but that's waiting, fixing itself
up, that whore is getting ready.

"ten-win-six," you say to the teller.

it's the beginning of a most pleasant afternoon.

my next university lecture will be
THE POSITIVE INFLUENCE
OF GAMBLING
AS A MEANS OF
DEFINING EXPERIENCE AS
SOMETHING THAT
CAN BE TOUCHED LIKE
A BOOK OF MATCHES OR
A SOUP SPOON.

yes, you think, going back to sit down,
it's true.

you never liked me

I let Reena give you a blow job
even though she was my wife,
I used to drive you to all your
poetry readings
and I have some photographs
of you in compromising
positions
with that hooker
but I've never shown them to
anyone.
Reena and I shared that motel
room with you down at Hermosa
Beach where you
tried to rape Robert's
widow
and I guess you don't
remember demanding that
the manager turn on the
swimming pool lights at
3:30 a.m.?
you tried to
drown him
afterwards
and I was the guy
who stopped him from
calling the cops.

and the time you wanted to
suicide
I was the one who gave you
those uppers.

you insulted my father and

his wife
and I was the one who talked
him out of killing
you; he was packing a
.45 . . .

and I drove you all over the
streets of Hollywood
for hours that day
until you found
your
car.

I'm sure
I've done many things for
you
that you don't even
remember,
still, you never
particularly
liked
me.

yet, I never asked
anything from you
before
but now there's
something
I need.
I've written
a frank memoir
about you
and our wild times together

and I want you
to give my publisher
your blessing.

o.k.?

by the way, I've been
following your
career.
I read your last
book.
it was
all right.

Reena sends her
love.

lemme know about
the blessing.

and don't you worry about
those
photographs.

your pal,
Benny.

our big day at the movies

it was during the Depression and the Saturday
matinee was for children and we stood in
long lines a good hour before the theater even
opened.
there was always a double feature but one
was an adult movie which they
featured first before we got to see our
Buck Rogers space movie.

the movie houses in those days were imposing
and clean with high curved ceilings and
fancy columns and the seats were big
and soft and the rugs in the aisles were red
and thick and there was always an usher or
usherette with a flashlight as we sat with jawbreaker
candy in our mouths and waited.

the adult movie was usually pure agony and
at the time there was an endless series of films
featuring Fred and Ginger, we saw movie after dreadful
movie of them dancing for hours, it was really
terrible, headache bad.
he wore shiny black shoes and a fancy coat
with long tails, the coattails flying
as he pranced and tap-danced.
he would leap on tables or dance along the
rail of a balcony far above the street below
and he had this little fixed smile on his
face, and she danced too, the blonde with
curly hair, she followed him in lockstep and
now and then he would toss her in the
air while she maintained a pleased and adoring expression
on her face.

there was always a minor plot in the movie, little bits of
trouble would arrive and to cure every-
thing he would begin dancing with
her, that was the answer, the solution.
sometimes they even kissed and we would
all look away and groan in disgust.

he was somebody to despise with his
sunken little face and thinning
hair and weak chin and sharp nose, always just
dancing, dancing, dancing
like someone gone mad.
I had never seen any man like that living
in our neighborhood;
our fathers would have run him off!
the lady wasn't so bad, she was
kind of pretty but stupid to fall
for a fellow like that.
sometimes those movies got so bad
that just for relief a couple of the boys
would get into a fight but the ushers
always quickly stopped it.

yes, it was agony watching those dancers
especially when they kissed
but it would finally end and then there
was a cartoon, Popeye, he'd eat a
can of spinach and punch out some
big ugly guy.
the ugly guy looked more like our fathers
than that dancing freak did.

our movie would come on then and
we'd really start to live! space
machines, space wars, the evil
Villain of Space and also his evil
Sidekick and Buck Rogers would
be captured and chained
in a dungeon somewhere
but somehow he always finally got
away.
some of the space guns were
terrific, they'd shoot rays
and people would just vanish
in a flash
and the beautiful rocket ships would
shoot through space and there were
tremendous battles between
Buck Rogers and the Villain
space ships (they were terrible like
hungry sharks and evil looking).
there was tension, fierce tension,
and then some new and horrible
development would suddenly take place
which Buck Rogers would some-
how overcome.
Buck always survived.
although he really had us worried
at times—like when he was
chained to this metal table with a
giant circular saw creeping closer
and closer.
there were many such narrow
escapes.

and then it would all be over
and we'd have to go back to our own lives,
to our parents, to whatever Depression dinner
they had managed to prepare.
but during those Saturday evenings
after the movies
we all felt different somehow,
strange, a little unreal, watching
our parents eat and converse,
our parents,
those people that had never experienced
anything exciting or real,
who seemed hardly alive,
they were almost as boring as
that kissing dancer with his flying
coattails
but not quite,
nothing could ever be
as bad as
that.

about competition

the higher you climb
the greater the pressure.

those who manage to
endure
learn
that the distance
between the
top and the
bottom
is
obscenely
great.

and those who
succeed
know
this secret:
there isn't
one.

fingernails

the nurse looked at
my face.
"are you a factory worker?"
she asked.
"no," I said.
"then this didn't
happen on the job?"
"no," I said, "I don't
work."
"how did this happen?"
the nurse asked.
"a woman," I explained,
"fingernails."
"oh," she laughed,
"well, fill out this
questionnaire. the doctor will
see you in a minute."

there was a long list of
strange questions:
have you ever been in a
mental institution?
have you had v.d.?
are your parents
alive?
do you resist
authority?
do you sleep on your
back?
are you sexually active?
what is your favorite
color?

if you had a chance,
would you take
it?

I felt that the nurse
had possibly given me
the wrong questionnaire.

there were a dozen more
questions of a
similar nature.

to all the questions
I answered,
I don't know.

the doctor came in,
glanced at the sheet,
put it down.

"you say a woman did
this?"

"yes."

"did she also bite you?"

"yes."

"what do you want?"

"a tetanus shot."

"when did you have your last
one?"

"I don't know."

the doctor grabbed my
face, started
picking at it.

some of the scab
came loose.
I began
bleeding.

"how does that feel?"
he asked.

"just fine," I told
him.

"o.k.," he said, "the
nurse will give you a
shot."

he began to walk out of
the room
then stopped and
turned. "by the way,
why did the woman
do this to you?"

"I wish I knew," I said.
"I really wish I knew."

the doctor left.
as the blood began to
trickle down and soak into
the collar of my
shirt I closed my
eyes and waited.

iron

we all go through it, those times
when we decide to angrily challenge everyone and
everything.
first we decide to get in shape.
we start pumping iron again,
slack muscles reluctantly responding.
then we go back to
hanging around the toughest
joints,
sitting quietly, waiting for
trouble, daring
trouble to show its face
and it finally arrives in the
form of some greasy
lowdown
hammerfisted
drunk.
a misunderstanding
ensues
and outside we go,
fist against bone,
sucking it up,
throwing punches straight from the
shoulder,
grunting,
sucking air,
shaking off the shots,
planting our feet,
the drunken screaming crowd
panting for somebody's
anybody's
demise.

you test the hammerfists
one by one
find some of them
wanting but,
fortunately, not
all.

the low-life ladies love
men who
fight.
and into your dim
room
they will now glide,
excited by your
dumb
valor
but soon
they will begin
to suck at your
independence;
with patience,
with guile,
they will try to claim you
permanently as their very own
making those
hammerfisted drunks
by comparison
look
harmless and
pale.

then you are sitting
around one night

in your cheap hotel
room
with
whoever
and she's speaking of her
unhappy childhood or about
the time she
hitchhiked alone through
the
untamed Amazon
and it hits you like a
kick in the gut:

what am I doing to myself
and why?

and you stop pumping
iron and
you dump her or better
yet, let her dump
you.

then you dump your misguided plan.

you abandon the proving
ground;
the proving ground
proves nothing
of importance.
it's all just
vanity stuffing its
own swollen
self.

you back away,
regroup.

it's easy.

a month later in some
public place
a boor and a bull
gives you the
elbow, a bit of a
shove.
he's in a hurry about
something and
you're slightly in his
way.
you catch his
eye.
"sorry, man," you
say, "you o.k.?"

he's puzzled, can't
make that out at
all.

fine.

a man has to circle,
finally come back to where
he was.

sometimes it takes a
while.
other times, perhaps, it can't

be done.

but since I have
finally accomplished this,
become reasonable and sane again,
the women have become
more beautiful and the
rooms larger and lighter,
not that I have searched for
either
but they have finally
found me.

of course, I still pump
iron at odd and
infrequent
moments;
old habits often die
as slowly
as do
old men.

extraterrestrial visitor

it was a hot afternoon in July.
her daughter was at the swimming
pool.
her son was at the roller rink.
we talked a while and then
gradually got down to it.
I was just
sliding in
when I thought I heard a
sound.
I pulled out and looked
around.
standing by the bed was this
black kid
about five years old.
he was barefoot.
"what do you want?" I
asked him.
"you got any empty bottles?"
he asked.
"no, I don't have any
empty bottles."
he left, disappointed.

"I thought the door was locked,"
she said, "that was Clovis's
little boy."
"Clovis's little boy?"
"yes."

I suppose it was.

small talk

I left the barstool to go
to the men's room.
I found that
there wasn't a urinal in
the men's room
just a toilet without a
lid
and in the toilet were
some ugly turds.
I kicked the flush-lever
with my foot but the
lever was broken.
I urinated while looking
away,
zipped up,
went to the sink: no
soap in the dispenser.
I turned the water
faucet on
and there was only
a trickle of
cold rusty liquid.
there were no paper
towels
and a large piece of glass
was missing
at the corner
of the mirror.

I left the men's room and
walked back to my stool,
sat down.

"you think Valenzuela's
going to sign with the
Dodgers?" the barkeep
asked me.

"doesn't matter to me,"
I said, "I don't like
baseball."

"you don't like baseball?"
he asked. "are you some kind of
queer?"

"not that I know of," I
told him. "give me another
beer."

as he bent over the cooler
I was privileged to view his
vast gross buttocks.
near the crotch of his
white pants was a large yellow
stain.

he came up with the bottle
flipped the lid off and
banged the beer down
in front of me.

"if you don't like baseball
what the hell do you
do in your spare time?"
he asked me.

"fuck," I said.

"dreamer," he answered
picking up my change and
walking to the cash
register.

"that too," I said.

I don't think he
heard me.

too sweet

I have been going to the track for so
long that
all the employees know
me,
and now with winter here
it's dark before the last
race.
as I walk to the parking lot
the valet recognizes my
slouching gait
and before I reach him
my car is waiting for me,
lights on, engine warm.
the other patrons
(still waiting)
ask,
"who the hell is that
guy?"

I slip the valet a
tip, the size depending upon the
luck of the
day (and my luck has been amazingly
good lately)
and I then am in the machine and out on
the street
as the horses break
from the gate.

I drive east down Century Blvd.
turning on the radio to get the result of that
last race.

at first the announcer is concerned only with
bad weather and poor freeway
conditions.
we are old friends: I have listened to his
voice for decades but,
of course, the time will finally come
when neither one of us will need to
clip our toenails or
heed the complaints of our
women any longer.

meanwhile, there is a certain rhythm
to the essentials that now need
attending to.
I light my cigarette
check the dashboard
adjust the seat and
weave between a Volks and a Fiat.
as flecks of rain spatter the
windshield
I decide not to die just
yet:
this good life just smells too
sweet.

work-fuck problems

I'm in Arizona
on a drive back from a horse stable
to the cabin where we're staying
air cooler blowing
boy and dog on floor laughing.

my dirty room back home is beyond the desert
many miles and a lifetime away
as I sit here inside my self
creating half-felt emotions.

the way to create art is to burn and destroy
ordinary concepts and to substitute them
with new truths that run down from the top of the head
and out from the heart.

this boy isn't mine this dog isn't mine the cabin
where I'm staying
isn't mine
but I own one-half of this typewriter.

after the drive back from the horse stable I find
the lady has gone to do her laundry
leaving me to burn and destroy
ordinary concepts.

well, I could be working in a factory instead
or driving a taxi
or picking tomatoes
if they'd hire me.

the boy walks in with a water gun,
squirts me.

"look, kid," I say, "I am trying to make a
living. I'm not good for anything else,
even picking tomatoes . . ."

the lady and I often argue about our WORK.
how are we going to get any WORK done
if we lie around and fuck day and night?

old Ez used to say DO YOUR WORK
but he fucked too.
me, I figure I can always WORK
but I can't always FUCK so I concentrate on FUCK
and let the WORK come when it can.

confidence, I have that, and a bit of talent.
but the lady is worried. she thinks I am going to
fuck us into the poorhouse.

creation is like anything else good:
you have to wait on it; ambition has killed more
artists than indolence.

I am not infected with ambition
I am quite content;
sitting across from the horse barn at
3 p.m. in the afternoon
I wait for Art to create me.

it's really pleasant

after 100 bad jobs
15 bad woman
and almost 60 bad years.

I listen to an opera on the radio
while outside the Indians and Mexicans bend in the hot sun
dreaming of wine bottles and revolution.

I too have been on their cross
now all I need to do is record the screams in my
memory
well enough
and wait for the lady to come back with her
laundry.

observations on music

I have sat for thousands of nights
listening to symphony music on the radio;
I doubt that there are many men my age
who have listened to as much classical music
as I have—
even those in the profession.

I am not a musicologist
but
I have some observations:
1) the same 50 or 60 classical compositions
are played over and over
and over again.
2) there has been other great music written that we
ignore at our peril.
3) the second movement of most symphonies is
only kind to insomniacs.
4) chamber music has every right to be energetic
and entertaining.
5) very few composers know how to END their
symphonies
but
most opening movements, like romance, have
early charm.
6) I prefer a conductor who inserts his own
interpretation rather than the purist who blindly follows
the commands of the master.
7) of course, there are always some conductors with so much ego and
"interpretation" that the composer
vanishes.
8) music is much like fucking, but some composers can't

climax and others climax too often, leaving themselves and the
    listener
jaded and spent.
9) humor is lacking in most so-called great musical
compositions.
10) Bach is the hardest to play badly because he
made so few spiritual mistakes.
11) almost all symphonies and operas could be
shorter.
12) too much contemporary music is written from the safe
haven of a university. a composer must still
experience life in its raw form in order to
write well.
13) music is the most passionate of the art forms;
I wish I had been a musician or a composer.
14) very few writers know how to END a
poem like this one
15) but I do.

fly boy

I was 8 years old and it wasn't going
well.
my father was a brute and my mother
was his assistant.
the boys in the neighborhood
disliked me.
I had a hiding place.
it was on the garage roof.
it was very hot up there
and I stripped down and sunbathed.
I decided to become bronzed and
strong.
I did push-ups and sweated in the
sun.
the roof was covered with white
pebbles which bit into my
skin,
but I never became bronzed, I only
burned to an idiot
red.
but I continued up there on the roof.
it was my hiding place.
then I got it into my head that I could
fly.
I don't know how it started, it was
gradual, the idea that I could
fly.
but as time went on the idea
became stronger and
stronger.
I wasn't sure why I wanted to
fly

but the idea of it possessed me
more and more.
I found myself perched on the
edge of the roof
several times
but I always stepped back.
then the afternoon came when I
decided that I would fly.
suddenly, I felt sure that I could.
I was elated.
I stepped to the edge of the roof,
leaped out and flapped
my arms.
I plunged down and hit
the ground, hard.
when I got up I found there
was something wrong with
my right ankle.
I could barely walk.
I limped into the house, made
it to the bedroom and got on
my bed.
an hour later my ankle was
swollen,
huge.
I took off my shoe.

my parents arrived home at
about this time.
"Henry, where are you?"
asked my father.

"I'm in here."

they both entered, my
father first and my mother
behind him.

"what happened to your
ankle, Henry?" my mother asked.

"an accident."

"an accident?" my father asked.
"what kind of accident?"

"I tried to fly, it didn't work."

"fly? how? from where?"

"from the roof of the garage."

"so, that's where you've been
hiding lately?"

"yes."

"do you realize this means a
doctor bill?
do you realize we don't have
any money?"

"I don't need a doctor."

"doctors cost money!
get in the bathroom!"

I got up and hobbled into the
bathroom.

"take down your pants!
your shorts!"

I did.

"doctors cost money!"

he reached for his razor
strop.
I felt the first bite of
it.
a flash of light
exploded in my
head.
he came down with the
strop again.
the sound of it against my
flesh was
horrible.

"fucking doctors!"

the strop landed
again
and then I knew why I had
wanted to

fly . . . to fly
right through the walls,
to fly
right out the
window,
to any place but
here.

unblinking grief

the last cigarettes are smoked, the loaves are sliced,
and lest this be taken for wry sorrow,
drown the spider in wine.

you are much more than simply dead:
I am a dish for your ashes,
I am a fist for your vanished air.

the most terrible thing about life
is finding it gone.

houses and dark streets

one of my greatest weaknesses is getting lost.
I am always getting lost, I have dreams about
getting lost, and this is why I fear going
to foreign countries: the possibility
of getting lost and not knowing the language.
I was once lost in the Utah wilderness for
nine hours but I also get lost on streets and freeways.
you'll see me pull into a gas station and ask:
"give me a couple of gallons of gas and
can you tell me where I am?"

I'll find the right freeway but then drive in the
wrong direction, drive fearfully
for many miles along with hundreds of people who
know exactly where they are going. I'll then
try going in the opposite direction, give up,
get off the freeway and
get lost again on a dark road with no streetlights and
silent, darkened houses:
many dark houses and a dark street
and no help in sight.
I'll turn on the car radio and sit and
listen to the friendly voices and the smooth
music—but that only increases my madness and fear.

there hasn't been a woman I have lived with
who hasn't received this phone call:
"listen, baby, I'm lost, I'm in a phone
booth and I don't know where I am!"
"go outside," they say, "and look for a
street sign."
I come back after a few minutes with the information and

they calmly tell me what to do.
I don't understand the instructions.
then there's much screaming back and forth.
"it's simple!" they scream.
"I CAN'T DO IT!" I scream back.

once after driving around for hours I
stopped and rented a motel room.
luckily there was a liquor store across the
street.
I got two fifths of vodka and sat up watching
tv
pretending that life was good and that I was
perfectly normal and in control of the situation.
I was finally able to sleep shortly after
opening the second bottle of vodka.

in the morning when I went to turn in my key
I asked the lady, "by the way, could you tell me
which way I go to get to L.A.?"

"you're in L.A.," she told me.

once leaving the Santa Anita racetrack
one evening
I swung off onto a side road to avoid the
traffic and the side road started to curve sharply and I
worried about that so I cut off onto another side road
and I don't know when it happened but the paved
street vanished and I was driving along on a
small dusty road and then the road started
climbing as the evening darkened into night and

I kept driving, feeling completely idiotic and
vanquished.
I tried to turn off the steep road but each
turn led me to a narrower road climbing even higher, and
I thought, if I ever see my woman again I'm going
to tell her that I'm a true subnormal,
that I must be restricted or kept in bed or that I should
be confined to an institution.

the road climbed higher and higher into the hills and
then I was on top of wherever it was and there was a lovely
little village brightly lit with neon signs and the language
on all the signs was Chinese! and then I knew that
I was both lost and insane!
I had no idea what it all meant, so I just kept driving
and then looking down I saw the Pasadena freeway
a thousand feet below: all I had to do was find
a way to get down there.
and that was another nightmare trying to
work my way down those steep streets lined with
expensive dark houses.
the poor will never know how many rich Chinese hide out
quietly in those hills.
I finally reached the freeway after another 45
minutes and, of course, I got on in the wrong
direction.

I don't like psychiatrists but I've often thought about
asking one of them about all this.
but maybe I already have the answer.

all the women I've lived with have told me the same thing:
"you're just a fool," they say.

the joke is on the sun

as the game continues you
should seek to say ever more clearly
what you truly
believe
even if what you truly
believe
turns out to be
wrong.

it can be a hazardous
and difficult
task.

but
if you can't laugh
at the impossible odds
we all endure as
we seek to understand
and know

then you will
surely sleep
restless
in the
coffin.

part 2

if I bet on Humanity
I'd never cash a ticket.

like a polluted river flowing

the freeways are a psychological
entanglement of
warped souls,
dying flowers in the dying hour
of the dying day.

old cars, young drivers,
new models driven by
aged men, driven by
drivers without licenses, by drunk
drivers, by drugged drivers,
by suicidal drivers, by super-cautious
drivers (the worst).

drivers with minds like camels,
drivers who piss in their seats,
drivers who yearn to kill,
drivers who love to gamble,
drivers who blame everybody else,
drivers who hate everybody,
drivers who carry guns.

drivers who don't know what
rearview
mirrors are for,
what the turn signals are for,
drivers who drive without brakes,
drivers who drive on bald tires.

drivers who drive slowly in the fast lane,
drivers who hate their wives or their husbands,
and want to make you pay for that.
unemployed drivers, pissed.

all these represent
humanity in general, totally enraged, demented,
vengeful, spiteful, cheap denizens of our culture, vultures,
jackals, sharks, suckerfish, stingrays, lice . . .

all on the freeway along with you
tailgating,
cutting in and out,
cheating themselves,
leering,
their radios blaring the worst music ever written,
their gas tanks nearly empty,
engines overheating,
minds over the next hill,
they don't know how to drive
or live,
they know less than a snail crawling home.

they are what you see every day
going from nowhere to nowhere,
they elect presidents, procreate, decorate their
Christmas trees.

what you see on the freeway is just what there is,
a funeral procession of the dead,
the greatest horror of our time in motion.

I'll see you there tomorrow!

girlfriends

the women of the past keep
phoning.
there was another yesterday
arrived from out of
state.
she wanted to see
me.
I told her
"no."

I don't want to see
them,
I won't see them.
it would be
awkward
gruesome and
useless.

I know some people who can
watch the same movie
more than
once.

not me.
once I know the
plot
once I know the
ending
whether it's happy or
unhappy or
just plain
dumb,
then

for me
that movie is
finished
forever
and that's why
I refuse
to let
any of my
old movies play
over and over again
for
years.

escape 1942

in San Francisco I watched them
march into the
shipyards
with their hard hats,
carrying their
lunch pails.

my father had written me
from Los Angeles: "If you
don't want to go to War
then work in the
shipyards, help your country
and
make some money."

I was insane.
I just sat in a small room and
stared at the walls.

now, many of those
shipyard workers
have found that
they were exposed to
asbestos
poisoning, and some of them
are now doomed to a slow
incurable
death.

one thing I found out
early
about my father's advice:
ignore it

without remorse
and you would avoid
many of life's
ordinary
agonies.

there would always
be
enough
of the other
kind.

a strange horse poem

yes, I once rode this strange horse everywhere
from 1940 until 1950
and his name was Nothing and we rode through New Orleans,
St. Louis, N.Y.C., east Kansas City, you name it, you name
the city—Atlanta, that was a real son of a bitch—and sometimes the
horse was named Greyhound, sometimes it was named
Greynothing, lots of young girls there, usually sitting with
        somebody
else, somebody dressed in a soldier's uniform looking
damned dumb to me but damned good to everybody else.
I could never get fucked, not that I wanted to, that was too
        impossible,
too far away, I just wanted to be included, to sit in a room
        somewhere with them,
watch the way their dresses moved as they crossed their legs,
but I always ended up with just a job and not a woman, a tiny job
somewhere in a ladies' dress shop or pushing dress samples or bolts
        of cloth
in a wooden cart through the streets of some city which name
I have now forgotten—up long ramps into tiny dark elevators with
        the cart
and the samples and the bolts of cloth, and once in the elevator you
        tugged on
a rope threaded through wooden spools, you yanked on the rope to
        stop and
start the thing, and there was hardly any light, you really had to
        look
hard to see the numbers of the floors written on the wall in
faded white chalk: 3, 6, 9, 10 . . . yank, stop . . . and push out to
be greeted by easily panicked old ladies and (forgive me) a fat
comfortable Jew with bright suspenders and an almost-
paternal glow, he looked better and kinder than any of us.

yes, I once rode this strange horse everywhere,
getting stuck briefly now and then in an all-yellow jail cell; the
yellow paint flecking off the bars showing gray paint underneath,
    always
a lidless toilet and a metal sink but the sink never worked,
it just dripped water out of a rusty faucet and you ducked your
head in there and sucked at the drops when you were thirsty.

I once stood in a Coca-Cola plant in Atlanta, damn it, not wanting
to be there, not wanting to be there at all, this man telling me, "I'm
    sorry, all
we have is one opening, $60 a month, we'd like to
offer you more but there's a government freeze on wages."

yes, I rode this strange horse everywhere and I want you
to know that for the insane and for other certain types
of people there are never any jobs anywhere and that even
in good times, in time of war, that there is a line
19 deep for the shittiest jobs in existence, and that
the hardest job to find is as a dishwasher or a
busboy or as a messenger boy for Western Union.

I rode this strange horse, I *was* this horse, so I want it known.
much later I was to meet women who would tell me, "Jesus,
    Chinaski,
why did you take all those terrible jobs when you easily
could have . . ."

I hate those women, hate those women who say
that, sitting in their plush offices, perhaps at some record company,
sniffing at drugs, purses full of pills, and them acting
ultra superior, taking me back to their apartments to fuck, and

expecting me to love and admire them when they had ridden
their horse exactly nowhere.

a cheap hotel in New Orleans: getting up at 6 a.m.
to go to work after a
night of 3 bottles of cheap wine, going out in the
dark, cold hall, leaving your room to look for a place to
shit and shave, but each little toilet taken, someone
in there shaving, and while you were
waiting, seeing rats as large as your hand scurrying
back and forth just before sunrise, running up and down
along the rusty corridor, you knew then that your father was
right, you'd always be a bum, you had no *drive*, and suddenly
the horse was very tired so you went back to bed, $4
left in your wallet, enough for some wine later and some change left
over.

I rode this strange horse and I rode this horse and I knew that
for some there would never be good times no matter
how good the times were, I knew that for some there
would never be something as simple as a woman, and for some
            never a
decent life, and finally dying like that, and maybe the
better for it?

you don't know how faithfully I rode this horse, you don't know
how I clashed with men who would fight to the end over a piece of
garbage, you don't know the terrible nights,
the night jobs of working with creatures with faces
as blank as paper bags and you trying
to find something, anything, behind that paper bag.

"Jesus, Chinaski, why didn't you find a job as a writer
or somethin'?" the ladies asked much later.

I checked out another job, shipping clerk, just a block from my
little room in Philadelphia, next to my favorite bar; I
got up early, took a bath, walked in and there
were 8 others waiting ahead of me
                    INCLUDING
one returning W.W.II vet in full uniform with *all* his medals
on.
well, they hired me because I lived just a block away and
they thought I'd never be late for work (but I was always
late for work).

this strange horse, you know, I've ridden him everywhere, I was
riding him just now when I accidentally smashed the glass out of the
bathroom window, my blood flung all up and down the stairway as I
chased him through the dark garden, throwing rocks,
blank naked under the blank moon, ripping plants up
by their roots, this strange horse, you know, he won't behave.
and I remember another time blandishing about with some
dopesters, "we'll cut you in, baby, you're the toughest guy we
know. we want you in."

but somehow that wasn't what I wanted either.
"listen," I told them, "I am really honored but I'm
just not interested in that sort of thing."

then I got on my strange horse and rode off, searching
as ever for the grapefruit dream.

the longest snake in the world

I parked outside, nice and shady, walked in.
I had a 2 p.m. appointment.
they took me right away, no waiting.
led me to a special room.
the doctor had a little smile.
the nurse looked bored.

"please take off your clothes," she said.

I stripped.

"have you ever had one of these examinations before?" the Dr.
asked.

"no."

"well, you're in for a treat."

"assume the position," said the nurse,
"on the chair."

there was a specially made
chair.
I climbed onto it.
they strapped my wrists down.
my ass was up in the air.

"it isn't going to hurt," said the
doc. "we're just going to take a look around
inside of you, there's a light on the
end of this coil and it lets us see inside, it even allows
us to take photos, we slide this tube right up into your
intestine."

is it too late to change my mind? I asked myself.

my mother-in-law had told my wife
that she had been through the same
procedure and that
there was nothing to it, nothing to worry
about.
she was always so helpful.

"now we're going to slide this up into your
intestine, you'll feel a little something but
don't worry . . ."

"right now?"

"right now. we're going in slowly . . . slowly . . ."

"you can breathe," said the nurse.

"thank you."

"this will be over so quickly you won't even
know we've done it,"
said the doc.

"but you'll bill me anyway . . ."

"the office will bill you. now, a little further . . ."

I imagined my white-haired mother-in-law crouched in
the same position, trying to act brave and
dignified.

a good girl, a good old girl.
nobody like her.

"umm hmmm," I heard the
doctor say.

"keep breathing," said the nurse.

"now we're coming out," said the doctor.
"coming out now, slowly . . ."

I had noticed the long tube coiled around the
large spool. there was a lot of intestine to examine in the
average human
being.

"we're finished," said the doctor.
"are you relieved?"

"oh, yeah!"

the nurse handed me a handful of
tissue.

"please clean yourself and get dressed."

I did that.
then I sat there waiting, staring at
the thick black tube coiled on the big
spool.

after a while the doctor walked back

in.
he was holding a piece of
paper.

"is 'Chinaski' Polish?" he
asked.

"it might be but I was born in
Germany."

"you now live in Palos Verdes?"

"San Pedro."

"San Pedro?
do you like it there?"

"doctor, for Christ's sake! do I have
cancer or not?"

"no, but you do have internal
hemorrhoids."

"that's fine with me."

"you should have them taken care
of.
we use rubber bands."

"rubber bands?"

"yes, we tie them in there and when
the bands dissolve the hemorrhoids
are gone."

"I don't think I'll bother."

driving back home
my ass didn't hurt at
all.
I punched on the radio, punched
in the lighter.
the lighter jumped out and I put it
to my cigarette.
there was a red light ahead.
I stopped.
there were 4 cars ahead of me
and a couple
behind.
and thankfully none of them knew a damned
thing about what had happened to
me and they never
would.

the niceties

I took my wife and mother-in-law
to dinner.
everything was all right until my mother-
in-law asked for
dessert.
I called the waiter over and
he brought her the dessert.
for the moment everything was
fine
but as he stood there
my mother-in-law looked up at
him
and mentioned that there was a
different name for that same
dessert
back east;
they called it something different
in Pennsylvania.
"oh," said the waiter, "are you
from Pennsylvania?"
that made my mother-in-law smile.
"yes," she said, "are you?"
the waiter said "no," that
he was from
Michigan.
my wife then said something about
Kalamazoo.
the waiter replied that he had a
sister in Kalamazoo.
"oh, do you go back there for
the holidays?" my mother-in-law
asked.
the waiter said, "no," he had

gone to Las Vegas instead.
then my wife asked him if he had won any
money in Las Vegas.
and the waiter said, "well,
actually, I did."
"oh, that's fine!" said my
mother-in-law.
then
somehow
the conversation got turned
back to Michigan, to one of the other
cities in Michigan and
the waiter said he had gone to
college there.
"oh," said my mother-in-law,
"one of my brothers went to that same school!"
"oh really?" said the waiter.
"he studied medicine there!"
said my mother-in-law.

about that time I decided to
tune out.
I could hear the sounds
but I allowed the content
to drift over my head.
it was very peaceful.

"HE'S ASKING YOU
SOMETHING!" I heard my wife
say.

I looked up.
the waiter was asking, "can I fill

your water glass?"
"no, thanks," I replied.

the waiter walked off and my
mother-in-law
dug her spoon into the
dessert,
lifted a little round
bite
and slid it into her
mouth.

she liked sweets and she was
from Pennsylvania.

time to water the plants and feed the cat

that woman took longer to dress than any woman
I had ever known.
one night first we made love, then looked at tv,
then we slept.
in the morning she was up, getting ready to
go to work.
I watched her through narrowed eyes; I checked her
buttocks and legs.
I got tired of that, it was about 7:30 a.m.
and I went back to sleep.
I awakened at 8:00, walked to the bathroom,
pulled open the door.
I screamed.
she was standing there naked in front of the mirror.
"Jesus Christ," I said, "I thought you had gone to
work!"
"do you want to use the bathroom?" she asked.
"no, it's all right."
I went back to bed. soon she came in and kissed me
goodbye with those big red lips and I smelled her good
perfume.
"phone me at work," she said, "it always cheers me
up."
after she left I went in and had a
shower. I found a Fresca in the refrigerator
drank that and went back to sleep.

I had a real hot dream: two women were fighting each other.
each wanted to give it all to me.
at first one would win for a while and
then the other would pull her off and have her turn
until the first one pulled her off and etc. . . .
I awakened. I was steaming.

then I got up and took a cold bath, got dressed,
then phoned her at work: "I gotta go home now,"
I told her.
"oh," she said, "just stay one more night."
"no," I answered, "I can't . . ."
"why?" she asked.
"I've got to go home, water the plants, feed the
cat," I explained.
"do that and come back. we'll have dinner out. I know
a great place," she said, "and it's on me."
"I've got to go home," I said, "I've got to rest."
"but," she said, "you rest all the time, you're
always in bed . . ."
"how about this weekend?" I asked. "suppose I see you
this weekend? it's already Thursday."
"well, all right, bad boy," she answered, "this
weekend then . . ."

I got into my Volks and drove away from
there.
a man in his late fifties has to
pace himself and
some women expect love to be
inexhaustible.

I'm flattered

the phone rang at 7 a.m.; I was in the kitchen;
I picked up the phone. "Hank?" "yes."
"how are you doing?" "fine. I was just feeding
the cats." "I'm calling you because
someone just phoned me and said, 'Hank died
last night,' then they hung up." "I'm all right, I'm
feeding the cats." "when I heard that I almost cried,
I was so shocked." "I'm flattered." "I'm calling from
New York," she said, "but when I get back I'd like to come
see you, I'll bring my new boyfriend." "sure, be glad to
see you."

that was the end of the conversation. I hung up.

all 5 cats were now looking at me, ten eyes.

there was a sixth cat upstairs. she ate upstairs
because the other cats terrorized her.

I spooned the cat food into the 5 dishes and placed
them on the floor. they went for it.

every 2 or 3 years somebody tells somebody else that I
have died and I then must tell that somebody else: no,
no, I'm just fine.

that's as bad as some woman named Helen who
told everybody that she had been married to me for several
years and hated every minute of it.

and what about the time somebody
who called himself Hank Chinaski went

up and down the aisles at a poetry reading shaking
people's hands?

I take the sixth bowl of food upstairs to the cat the other
cats terrorize and I set it down and she goes for it.

then I go back to bed with my real wife who is still
asleep and I wonder why that person had phoned this
other person to tell them that I was dead?

it didn't anger me. I just wondered.

I was on the minds of a lot of people. it was my own
fault for being such an easy writer to read.

sometimes it seems that only the disabled
and insane like to read my books,
the ones who can't quite grasp
Chaucer.

the sixth cat finishes its meal, jumps up on the bed,
settles against my left flank and begins to
lick
lick
lick
lick
lick,
head
bobbing
bobbing
bobbing.

the beginning of
another
perfect
day.

neither Shakespeare nor Mickey Spillane

turn back the years, look you're back
at the beginning again,
living on a candy bar a day in the cheapest
room in town—
trying to be a writer, not a great writer but
somebody who gets checks for what he writes
and lives on those checks
and doesn't need an automobile or a
girlfriend and needn't go to work each day,
just be a writer, pumping it out, day after
day, day and night, words hot on the paper,
at 2½ cents a word, 5 cents a word, anything at all
would be enough,
writing stories for the pulp magazines, stories for
the sex mags (great escapades of
a fantastic fucker) and at the same time sending out your
serious stuff to *Poetry, a Magazine of
Verse.*

the candy bar was the bread and your blood
was the wine and the long-legged, long-haired
girls were chased away so you could get the
Word down for the pulps, for the sex rags, for the
Atlantic Monthly and *Harper's* and
Esquire and *The New Yorker,* those cold
fuckers who kept sending it all back while printing only
clever careful crap.

young young young, only wanting the Word,
going mad in the streets and in the bars,
brutal fights, broken glass, crazy women screaming in
your cheap room,

you a familiar guest at the drunk tank, North
Avenue 21, Lincoln Heights.

sifting through the madness for the Word, the line,
the way,
hoping for a check from somewhere,
dreaming of a letter from a great editor:
"Chinaski, you don't know how long we've been
waiting for you!"

no chance at all.

it finally came down to less words after years of 5 short
stories and 20 poems a week, it came down to less
words and more wine and more crazy women and
more broken glass and screaming, vengeful landlords
and, of course, finally the police.

you young, taller, stronger in the mountains in your
mind, stinking drunk, screaming
"SCREW YOU GUYS! I'M A GENIUS!"

handcuffs snapped on in back, always too tight, the
steel cutting into the wrists, the
sharp brutal pain.
"shut up, buddy, or I'll shut you up."

turn back the years and there you are,
36 years ago,
and a greater more interesting time
was never to be had.
you had a faith then that is missing
now.

but the hardest thing, the current woman, slobbering
drunk, hair in face, crying . . .

"let her go fellows, she didn't do anything,
you don't want her,
she was just along for the ride."

"god damn you, shut up!" from the cop,
shoving you through the door, down the
stairway fast
where it took all your effort not to fall
headlong, which was what he
wanted, hands cuffed behind you, you would
be unable to break the fall . . .

you broke into song then:
"My Heart Is a Hobo . . ."

and you heard the angry cop curse in the
dark
as you were led away.

all you wanted was 2½ or 5 cents a
word.
son of a bitch, you ached so hard to be a writer
of any kind.

why didn't they understand?

show business

Marty, listen to me, *all* the stars are
gonna be there!
I know there's no money in it for you!
but it's good public relations!
the public LOVES these AIDS
BENEFITS, Marty!
it lets them know you got
heart, it lets them know you
got soul!
ask any P.R. man!
they've all got their clients doing
it!
look at Sammy D.! he's your
buddy, you think he gives a FUCK
if somebody dies of AIDS?
he knows the payoff will come
later
when he's doing his next big gig!
get with it, Marty!
everybody's doing it!
watch out or the public is going
to ask, "how come Marty Mellon
ain't appeared at no AIDS
BENEFITS?"
that's DEATH, Marty!
for YOU!
GOT IT?
HUH?
ATTA BABY!
YOU JUST ABOUT SCARED THE
SHIT OUT OF ME!
now, the next one is set for

June 20th, I'll put you down for
that, every asshole in town is gonna
be there . . .

pop!

this idiot's wounded flower
dangles peacefully,
but boy, what a war!
just like all the other wars
but each new one seems more and more
the same as the one before!
nothing is very new
as I sit here arranging
these impossible words,
sifting out all the impossibilities.
this is a *denouement*, baby, because
you told me that you were different
than the others
but how different?
you mean you don't piss behind
boulevard signboards?
I haven't forgotten to water the little
plants around the doorway
and I'm left here alone with our cats, three of
them, six eyes looking, they are
walking bellies, I feed them,
drink, type about all this,
there can be nothing great said
here, nothing even decent, nothing even
understandable, and I'm just now pulling
another wine cork with my
yellow corkscrew, and that's where
I got this title.

the interview

I read it all.
the poet went on and on
talking about the value of
workshops.
this poet taught at a
university.
believed in teaching poets in
prison,
and teaching poets in the schools,
high schools,
reading his poems there,
bringing the word.
this poet had studied under
C. and R. and O.
yes, this poet always carried
a notebook
to capture impressions
at odd moments
else they would be forgotten.
yes, this poet revised his stuff
many times.
as much as six revisions per
poem.
this poet had been awarded
grants and
prizes.
during dry periods this poet hiked
or rode his bicycle.
the masses, said this poet,
were hungry for poetry.
the reason the books didn't
sell was not that poetry itself
was insufficient but that the

masses were sadly unaware of
it.
it was our duty to awaken the
people he said, it was our responsi-
bility, etc.

I dropped the magazine to the
floor, got up, walked to the
bathroom
and had one of my best
bowel movements in
several years.

re-union

when you left I thought you'd never
return and finally I got to feeling good
about that.

now it's starting all over
again

right here
right now.

I watch
the pyramids stand by quietly as the monkey eats his
fleas.

somehow
once again
we seem to be as
content as a package of
peanuts

bleached by the sun
and then

caught like
a
ringing bell.

Genius unfettered

Mr. Colskey studied under Bartmouth at
the Zale Institute,
then studied with the legendary
Randall Steel at
Milestone.
he was assistant conductor under
Frank Zellenstein
for 11 years
with the Brighton-on-Hudson
Orchestra.
when Mr. Zellenstein retired in
1955
Mr. Colskey
took over the baton.
besides his directorial duties
Mr. Colskey has found time
for his own
compositions,
the best known being
his Symphony in Two Movements,
The Coffin, the Burial,
a lengthy work of almost total
silence.
other works are his piano
sonata,
One for Grandma's Canary,
and his work for solo flute,
Canard Base.
there is also his
daring operatic overture,
*Photo of a Dog's Tail
Wagging.*

Mr. Colskey has delighted
audiences for half-a-
century now.
eccentric in approach and
manner,
difficult, reproachful,
demanding, errant at times,
still, he has left his mark
on the world of
music.
seven times married
and with some 14 children
he still presents
an ominous, stirring
and heroic
figure upon the
podium.

tonight Mr. Colskey is
to present the
World Premiere
of his tone poem,
*Up Your Aspen
Dream.*

parts of this introspective
score have previously appeared
in Mr. Colskey's only
Cello Concerto,
Angels Are Green.

Mr. Colskey is now appearing
on stage
carrying his baton
to the applause of the
audience
here in
Sibling Hall.

now he is facing forward,
smiling,
and he has taken out his
penis and is
urinating!
the audience is
silent and frankly
stunned!

he finishes, zips
up, then walks off
stage.

we are afraid
Mr. Colskey has dealt
his career
a final, fateful
blow

as the orchestra now
strikes up and begins
to play
Anton Bruckner's

*Symphony #6
in A Major.*
without Mr.
Colskey.

Bob

the other day we were in a
bookstore in the mall
and my woman said, "look, there's
Bob!"

"I don't know him," I said.

"we had dinner with him
not too long ago," she said.

"all right," I said, "let's get
out of here."

Bob was a clerk in the store
and his back was to us.

my woman yelled, "hello, Bob!"

Bob turned and smiled, waved.
my woman waved back.
I nodded at Bob, a very
delicate blushing fellow.
(Bob, that is.)

outside my woman asked, "don't you
remember him?"

"no."

"he came over with Ella. re-
member Ella?"

"no."

my woman remembers everything.

I don't understand it, although
I suppose it's polite
to remember names and faces
I just can't do it
I don't want to carry all those
Bobs and Ellas and Jacks and Marions
and Darlenes around in my mind. eating and
drinking with them is difficult en-
ough.
to attempt to recall them at will
is an affront to my well-
being.

that they remember me is
bad enough.

bearclaw morning

I was sitting at a café counter
having a couple of eggs
while waiting for the locksmith
to fix the lock on the door
of my car.

the day before
at the racetrack parking lot
someone had jimmied open the door
and ripped out the radio and
the stereo.

I didn't miss the radio and
the stereo
but I didn't like
the big hole in the dash
with all the wires
sticking out
like spaghetti.

locks never stop the pros
from getting in, but anyhow
as I was eating
a little dark-skinned man
in his late fifties
sat down next to me and
ordered a bearclaw and a
coffee.

he looked over at me.
"the employment office is
closed," he said.

"yeah?"

"yeah, it's that damn Reagan.
it's closed down. you gotta go
all the way to Wilmington
now. it's a dirty town.
they don't even use
street sweepers."

"gimme another coffee, please,"
I told the waitress.

"sure, honey," she said
bringing the pot, "I guess you're
out of cream?"

"don't be funny," I
said.

"you gonna go to Wilmington?" the
little guy asked me.

"my car's in for repairs,"
I said.

"how ya gonna get a job?" he asked.
"ya gotta go all the way to Wilmington."

"I don't need a job," I said.

I was watching the two cooks, there
was a new cook and an old cook and the

new cook had an order for a ham sand-
wich and he started to slice into the
baked ham.
the old cook grabbed his arm: "no,
no . . ." he reached under the counter
and came up with a pressed ham patty:
"give 'em this."

"you look like you need a job,"
the little man said.

"I'm a gambler,"
I said.

"what?"

"horses, mainly. but I also beat the
point spread, basketball and
football. I loaded
up on Tyson in the
big fight and I pimp in
Gardena a little bit."

"how do you learn all that stuff?"
he asked.

I just smiled at him
picked my bill up and laid the tip
down.

as I stood at the counter paying
my bill

I flashed some green and
stuck a toothpick
into my mouth.

I picked up my change and when
I put my wallet away
I didn't stick it
into a rear pocket but
into the left front pocket,
carefully.

as I opened the door
two little old white-haired ladies
entered.

"good morning, girls," I said in a
soothing voice.

outside
I stood a moment
quietly in the sun
and stretched
not thinking about a god-
damned thing.

then I decided that I'd
better go see about the
door lock on the driver's
side.

but first I stretched again
leisurely
in the sun

while glancing down at a
paper rack full of *The
Wall Street Journal.*

refreshed, I turned and
started walking back to
the locksmith's place.

death and transfiguration

left the place with the girlfriend screaming.
then on the freeway
I look back and there he is:
a cop on a bike with his red lights
flashing.
I pull over, he writes me up, then
I continue,
make the track,
lose the first 8 races,
make my last
bet and leave,
drive back on in,
pull into the driveway.
there's the girlfriend standing in the
doorway.
she waves, smiles
like nothing happened.
I get out of the car, limp slowly toward the
door.
I'll phone to see
how I did in the
9th.

warriors in this place

I see a brutal and vapid face—
it's astonishing!
look, it's on a head and the head is
attached to a body and now the body
is walking out of the
room.

at least the face is gone now and I pick
up my chopsticks and contemplate:
why did that man bother me
so?
is it that I feel the waste of centuries?
the waste of nothing having gone forward?
or does the son of a bitch just make me
sick for reasons I don't understand?

I need more balance, a more distanced
perspective.
I should accept what is.
nightmares are a part of existence.

he comes back into the restaurant,
walks behind me down to the end of the
room, reaches his table,
stops.
he looks back at me.

it's a stare-down.
we are locked in a stare-down.
finally a friend says something to him and
he pulls out his chair and sits
down.
enemies forever have met in a

sushi bar.
I wish for his death as he wishes for
mine.

I take my chopsticks,
smile,
and pick up a
California roll.

a sickness?

yes, I'm a Romantic, overly sentimental,
something of a hero worshiper,
and I do
not apologize for this.
instead, I revere Hemingway,
at the end of his endurance,
sticking the
barrel of the gun into his trembling
mouth;
and I think
of Van Gogh slicing off part of his ear
for a whore
and then blasting
himself away in the
cornfield;
then there was Chatterton drinking rat
poison (an extremely painful way to die
even if you are a
plagiarist);
and Ezra Pound dragged through
the dusty streets of Italy in a cage
and later confined to a
madhouse;
Celine robbed, hooted at, tormented by
the French;
Fitzgerald who finally quit drinking only to drop dead
soon thereafter;
Mozart in a pauper's grave;
Beethoven deaf;
Bierce vanishing into the wastelands of Mexico;
Hart Crane leaping over the ship's rail and
into the propeller;
Tolstoy accepting Christ and giving all his

possessions to the
poor;
T. Lautrec
with his short, deformed
body
and perfectly developed
spirit,
drawing everything he
saw
and more;
D. H. Lawrence
dying of TB
and preparing his own Ship of Death
while writing his
last
great poems;
Li Po
setting *his* poems
on fire
and sailing them down the
river;
Sherwood Anderson dying
of peritonitis
after swallowing a
toothpick
(he was at a party
drinking
martinis
when
the olive went in,
toothpick and
all);

Wilfred Owens killed
in the first Great War
while
saving the world for
Democracy;
Socrates drinking
hemlock with a
smile;
Nietzsche gone mad;
De Quincey addicted to opium;
Dostoevsky standing blindfolded before a
firing squad;
Hamsun eating his own
flesh;
Harry Crosby committing
suicide hand in hand with his
whore;
Tchaikovsky trying to
evade his homosexuality
by marrying a female
opera star;
Henry Miller, in his old
age, obsessed with
young Oriental
girls;
John Dos Passos going
from fervent left-winger
to ultraconservative
Republican;
Aldous Huxley taking
visionary
drugs and

reaping imaginary
riches;
Brahms in his youth,
working on ways
to build a powerful
body
because he felt that
the mind
was not
enough;
Villon barred from Paris,
not for his ideas
but rather because he was a
thief;
Thomas Wolfe who felt he couldn't
go home again
until
he was
famous;
and Faulkner:
when he got his morning mail,
he'd hold the envelope up
to the light
and if he couldn't see
a check in there
he'd throw it
away;
William Burroughs who shot and
killed his
wife
(he missed the apple
perched

on her
head);
Norman Mailer knifing *his*
wife; no apple
involved;
Salinger not believing
the world was worth writing
for;
Jean Julius Christian Sibelius,
a proud and beautiful man
composer of powerful music
who after his 40th year
went into hiding and was seldom
seen
again;
nobody is sure who
Shakespeare
was;
nightlife killed Truman
Capote;
Allen Ginsberg becoming a
college
professor;
William Saroyan marrying the
same woman twice
(but
by then
he wasn't going anywhere
anyhow);
John Fante being sliced away
bit by bit
by the surgeon's knife

before my very
eyes;
Robinson Jeffers
(the proudest poet of them all)
writing
begging letters to those in power.

of course, there's more
to tell
and I could go
on and on
but even I
(the Romantic)
begin to
tire.

still, these men and women
—past and present—
have created and are creating
new worlds for
the rest of us,
despite the fire and despite the ice,
despite the
hostility of governments,
despite the ingrown distrust of the masses,
only to die
singly
and usually
alone.

you've got to admire them all
for the courage,
for the effort,

for their best and at their
worst.

some gang!
they are a source of light!
they are a source of joy!

all of them
heroes you can be
grateful for
and admire from afar
as you wake up
from your ordinary dreams
each morning.

a fine night

there's one, she's walking along looking
straight ahead, sticking out her thumb,
she's fat, no, I won't want it, let her
be somebody else's trouble.
in my rearview mirror I see somebody else pull
over and she climbs in.

VIKING MOTEL, Vacancy, I park, a
woman talks to me through protective glass:
$28.
fine.
it comes to $30.10 with tax.

room 12, on the end.
I go in. box of a room, lumpy
double bed, torn blue bed-
spread, I yank it to the floor.

the tv is black-and-white,
12 inch, I turn it on, turn it
around to face the wall.

I strip down, do some shadow
boxing, decide to shower:
2 tiny pieces of soap and
the shower head is built for
a guy 4 feet tall.
I gyrate about, thinking,
the only meaningful thing about
the South is that they lost
the Civil War and still can't
accept it.

I leave the shower, go
to bed and lie there
wet.

I pick up the phone, dial a
number.
"where are you?" she asks.
"when you get personal you get
overbearing," I tell her.
I hang up.

I find a matchbook in the
ashtray. it tells me that
I am close to the beaches
and

4 MILES SOUTH OF
LOS ANGELES AIRPORT

I could fly to Peru.
I could fly to China.

I sit up on the edge of
the bed
dig the corkscrew
out of the paper bag
along with the first bottle
of *petite sirah*
unpeel a long strip of red
cellophane
twist corkscrew into cork
yank it out.

sometimes a man has to take refuge in
a motel room
to save his
god-damned soul.

riots

I've watched this city burn twice
in my lifetime
and the most notable event
was the reaction of the
politicians in the
aftermath
as they
proclaimed the injustice of
the system
and demanded a new
deal for the hapless and the
poor.

nothing was corrected last
time.
nothing will be changed this
time.

the poor will remain poor.
the unemployed will remain
so.
the homeless will remain
homeless

and the politicians,
fat upon the land, will thrive
forever.

Venice Beach

the lost and the damned
the wounded and the intellectual
the boozed and the debauched
the negative and the
uninspired
and the police
and the police
and the police.

the con job

the ground war began today
at dawn
in a desert land
far from here.
the U.S. ground troops were
largely
made up of
Blacks, Mexicans and poor
whites
most of whom had joined
the military
because it was the only job
they could find.

the ground war began today
at dawn
in a desert land
far from here
and the Blacks, Mexicans
and poor whites
were sent there
to fight and win
as on tv
and on the radio
the fat white rich newscasters
first told us all about
it
and then the fat rich white
analysts
told us
why
again
and again

and again
on almost every
tv and radio station
almost every minute
day and night
because
the Blacks, Mexicans
and poor whites
were sent there
to fight and win
at dawn
in a desert land
far enough away from
here.

looking back

now
I can't believe myself then:
in the bars
attempting to pick up
the lowest
women:
sagging stockings,
rouged cheeks,
deathly mascara,
yellow-toothed,
rat-eyed,
bellowing hyena
laughter
and when I was
successful
(peacock proud)
I was Attila,
I was Alexander the
Great,
I was the toughest
roughest guy in
town—
Bogart, Cagney,
Gable, all rolled up into
one.

and worse,
I can't understand myself then:
continually choosing the biggest
meanest bastard in the bar
to come and fight
in the alley,
to get myself clubbed by

blows I didn't
see coming.
my brain jumping inside
my skull,
seeing shots of
color, flashes of
light, feeling my
mouth fill with blood,
sensing my body
sprawled
on the pavement,
only to get up and rush
forward again with my
tiny hands.
there was many a
fight when I hardly
landed a
punch.
I was a laugh a
minute and the crowd
had all
night
to watch.
I'd get my beating
and they'd get their
jollies.

my face was never completely healed.
I walked around
with a fat
lip, a black
eye, a nose that

hurt.
I developed bone-
spurs on my
knees from falling so
hard
and so often.
yet a couple of nights
later
I'd be looking
for a new
meaner
bastard
to challenge.

but even harder to believe
now
was when finally
through some unexpected
stroke of luck
I did occasionally win
one
I was accorded no
cheers, no
accolades.
my stripe, my function
in that strange little world
was to
lose.
I was the guy from out of
town
and not even of the
neighborhood.

the strangest most hateful
nights were after I had finally
won,
sitting alone at the end
of the bar
as that gang laughed and
talked it up
as if I wasn't even
there.

but when I lost they loved me
and the drinks came
all night
long.

so when I won I lost
and when I lost I
won.

and
looking back
it is hard for me to believe
some of the women
I ended up
shacking with.
they all had good bodies,
great legs,
but the faces!
the faces were faces from
hell!
they were all fair in bed
(in spite of rather a general
indifference to sex)

but
they had ways of flattering
me.
I was younger
than they were
and
more open to the
dream.

but Christ, they *were* good at
locating my wallet,
after a day or two
or a week or two
they'd vanish
with all my money
to leave me
scrabbling for rent,
food, sanity and that
infamous
lost
dream.

only to reappear again!
knocking on my 3 a.m.
door
as if nothing had
happened:

"hi! how've you been?"

back from robbing some
other poor son of a
bitch.

and worse,
I'd let them back in,
liking the look of the leg,
the general madness of it
all,
to drink with them then,
to hear their new sad
stories,
to let the dream seep
back in . . .
after all, where was I to find
a real lady?
down at the public library?
or at the opera house?

"come on in, baby, show me
some leg and let's hear
your story.
and come on, have a
drink!"

I had no plans.
I had no idea of what I was
doing,
where I was
going,
the world was a strange and
oppressive
place.
a man had to have guts
to shove on through.
everybody was so sad,

defeated,
subservient.

"tell me all about it, baby!"

but in spite of everything
I liked myself with my tiny
hands and my pockmarked
monkey face.
I liked sitting in my
shorts and my undershirt,
the undershirt torn and
dirty and full of cigarette
burns and wine stains.
I had muscular arms
and great powerful legs
and I loved to walk the rug
with my whore watching
while I spouted
inanities and
insanities.

I was hot stuff.
I was young stuff.
I was a fool
and I loved playing the
fool.

"o.k., baby show me
more leg!
more!
your talk bores me!

lift your skirt higher!
hold it there!
not too high!
I don't want to see
everything!
let me imagine it!"

looking back, it all couldn't have been much
better.

what a lovely
fucking
time
it was.

the love poems of Catullus

she read his poems
she read them to the men waiting in her bed
then tore them up
laughing
and fell on the bed
opening her legs to the nearest convenient
cock.

but Catullus continued to write love
poems to her
as she fucked slaves in back
alleys, and
when they were together
she robbed him while he was
drunk,
mocked his verse and his
love,
pissed on his
floor.

Catullus who
otherwise
wrote brilliant
poems
faltered under the spell of
this wench
who
it is said
as she grew old
fled from him
begat a new life upon a far isle
where she ended up a
suicide.

Catullus was like
most poets:
I understand
and forgive as I
re-read him:
he knew
as death approached
that it's
better to start out with a
strumpet than to end up
with one.

dream girl

when the sun comes up in the morning
(I sleep on my belly so it's always from my left)
I awaken to
that lovely golden light
and
I'm usually alone
and I sometimes (but not always) wonder why the most
beautiful woman in the world is not sleeping there next to
me?
I deserve her, I think, I deserve
her.

then I get up
go to the bathroom
splash water on my face

look into the
mirror

shudder a bit
in
disbelief

then

go sit down on
the ivory
stool

let it all
go

except for the
reality

which

no amount
of
efficient
modern
plumbing
can

whirl
away.

empties

we emptied wine bottles as if they were
thimbles
and our 4 a.m. arguments had caused us to be evicted from
apartments all over the city
but our biggest problem was the disposal of all the
empties.
we were afraid the landlord would be tipped off by his
trash cans, that he'd realize there were two serious drunks
among his tenants
so we snuck some of the empties into neighborhood
trash cans
but we still had many leftovers
which we hid in our room
for weeks on end
in cartons and bags until we were overwhelmed by
the accumulation.
finally
upon a given night
after drinking for a few hours
we'd sneak the bags and boxes
down the back stairway and
into our old car
(luckily, a sedan)
and we'd get in
the floor in back
stacked high with
bag and box upon bag and box
and the back seat also jammed with
boxes and sacks of empties
rising up against the windows
so that visibility was almost
impossible
while in front

at our feet sat the last of
the boxes and bags of
empties
where they shifted and slid
getting in the way as I worked the
clutch, the brake, the gearshift
while, of course, between us, we also carefully preserved
a couple of *fulls*
at the ready.
such a clinking and clanking of empties as we drove
in the moonlight!
driving slowly up into the Baldwin
Hills
we were
terrified that the police might stop
us
and insist that we spend
at least a couple of days in
jail;
our journey took us over
unpaved roads
in that old car
we knew might quit at any
moment;
afraid to be noticed
I'd cut the headlights
and drive in the moonlight
the forest of silent oil wells
indifferent to us
and at last
we'd get to where the road was
both rocky *and* muddy

and I'd say,
"THIS IS IT!"
then
as if the very searchlight of
God was focused on me
I'd leap out and begin throwing
sacks and boxes of empties into the
throbbing dark,
over the nearest cliff
hearing them tumble and crash
along with the sound of breaking glass.
I'd grab faster and faster
sweating, dizzy and sick as
I'd hurl the empties into the empty
night
until the car was
cleaned out.
then
she would look at
me and say,
"Jesus Christ, did we drink all
that?"
and I'd smile
get in
start the car
and it felt so good to be rid of
all those empties!
all that baggage!
and I'd disengage the gears
to save on fuel
and we'd glide down out of the
hills

unnoticed by everything and
everyone.
she'd hand me a fresh
hit
and I'd pass it back
and
she'd say,
"geez, don't you feel
better?"
and I'd answer, "yeah, how much
we got left?"
she'd hold up the
bottle. "enough to get us
home."

it was a hollow, temporary victory that
only someone like us could
appreciate.
"we got another bottle at the
apartment?" I'd ask.
"maybe 2, maybe 3," she'd
reply,
and we'd head back to our
place
(a place we now hoped would remain ours
for a while).
we'd done what we could to
preserve our status as decent
sober citizens
and although we knew that time was always
running out on us
in every way

we tried our best to preserve that illusion
because we knew no one else would ever
understand the way we really were, nor did we
expect them
to.

the landlady

all you got living above you is a boy.
the room is $100 and you pay the
utilities. Connie want a
cookie? don't she have a nice
face? you're not afraid of dogs, are
you? I thought not. you
been living very long in this
neighborhood? I been here since
1922. I remember President Harding, his
big hat. a real
gentleman. you know Ernie Bowers? he's been
living in this neighborhood all his
life!
you got two couches.
you get a visitor and
she can sleep on one couch and
you on the
other. they unfold into
beds. there's a kitchen and your own
toilet. all you got living above you is a
young boy, that's all.
he comes home from work
listens to a little music and then
goes out and eats. Connie, do you want a
cookie? Connie, have a cookie!
she's *so* sweet. she wakes me every morning
to go out and do her shame. she wakes me with
her paw. *so* sweet. have a cookie,
Connie. old Ernie Bowers . . . he's 82, he talks mainly
to himself now, I saw him on the corner
yesterday. did you know he used to double for
Rudolph Valentino in the movies? and he's also a mimic.
he used to look just like

Rudy. he carries these old photos of
himself to prove it. he's a real good mimic too.
you ought to see him
do Dean Martin . . .

about the mail

I get more and more letters
and they generally fall into one of two
camps:

one, from ladies who say they like my
writing,
and then they tell me the bare facts
of their life and they are always careful to
mention their *age*, usually anywhere from
18 to 35.
one lady even sent me the key to her
house
but since it was in Australia
I threw it
away.

one 18-year-old keeps writing, wondering why
I don't answer.
she says, "are you afraid to
fuck me?"

that's not what I'm afraid
of.

the second kind of letter comes from
men, men who are going crazy on the
job, or going crazy because of a wife or girlfriend
or family and
some of the men might actually be crazy, because
they write from
madhouses, while many others write from
jail.

most infer that my books have helped them
get through some tough times, at least
for the moment.

frankly, I always thought that
my writing was for the purpose of
keeping *me* from going
under

but it appears I've helped any number
of others.

well, being helped happened to
me too:

there was
Celine
Dostoevsky
Fante
early Saroyan
Turgenev
Gorky
Sherwood Anderson
Robinson Jeffers
e. e. cummings
Blake
Lawrence
and
many
others

and
if I can pass some courage on

to my correspondents

then the royalties
the luck
the satisfaction
and the
honor
are
legitimately
mine

in that
order.

have you ever pulled a lion's tail?

I knew a girl in a brownstone
and I was a warehouseman
with a forehead pulled down over
my eyes
trying to figure out where I was at.

and one night a lion got loose
and we were in the park
and I saw it first
and I saw it later,
looking back over my shoulder,
I saw it mauling my poor girl,
and then I felt bad
and ran back
and pulled at its tail
and threw rocks
until a cop came up and shot
the thing,
and she was a shock of blood,
didn't know who I was
and they put her in an ambulance
and then she was gone.

I walked down to the center of town
to the penny arcade
and I played all the games,
the basketball game, the golf game,
the soccer game, saw an old
movie, tested my strength,
and then I phoned the hospital
and she was still alive,
but no visitors,
and I went home and there was

half a 5th left
and I opened a can of roastbeef hash
and some pickled beets,
but I couldn't get over how funny
his tail felt.
have you ever pulled a lion's tail?

I only ate half the hash
and went to bed and worked on the 5th.
it was Sunday night and I kept thinking
I probably would have been in her by now
and now maybe she won't look so good
if she makes it.

why don't they leave the lions in Africa?
you can't blame the lions.

I finished the 5th, and phoned Vicky.
she was from someplace in New Hampshire,
a little tall
with a squint eye,
but what did it matter?
the evening
was still
young.

who needs it?

see this poem?
it was
written without drinking.
I don't need to drink
to write.
I can write without
drinking.
my wife says I can.
I say that maybe I can.
I'm not drinking
and I'm writing.
see this poem?
it was
written without drinking.
who needs a drink now?

probably the reader.

tight black pants

she was a schoolteacher and she wore tight black pants
and she sat over by the fire
and talked about how interesting children were,
how she liked her job with the little ones;
I had brought a 6-pack and Harry went for another one;
she was one of Harry's girls, she was 38,
and then she went for a 6-pack and came back
and once while Harry was out in the kitchen
I kissed her on the way to the crapper.
I came back and we talked some more
and then I decided I had better leave her with Harry,
and I got out, pulled out of the driveway,
and there was Harry in there with her
down by the seashore
playing Shostakovich's 5th symphony
and I was out of it,
out of trouble, uninvolved,
she had her little ones and she had Harry and Harry had
her, and somehow
I felt I was the only winner
driving down Pico Blvd.
past a McDonald's
it was a quiet easy night,
controlled, definite and meaningful.
poor Harry would get all that ass;
the only thing that would save him now was for California
to fall into the
ocean.

the weirdest day

I went to the baseball game
with Jane.
we each had a bottle with us
and were also drinking beer
on the side.
it was back in the old days when the
L.A. Angels played at
Wrigley Field.
anyhow, we got to
arguing
and Jane left.
I never stop women when they
want to
leave.
I figure if they are dumb enough
to leave me
they don't deserve
me.

anyhow, I kept drinking and
got to feeling
rancorous.
before the pitcher threw each
ball
I would shout what
I thought was
going to happen.
I would either yell
"STRIKE!" or
"BALL!" or
"IT'S A HIT!"
and I was a big guy

and young and mean
so nobody
said anything.

the strangest thing was that
I called everything correctly.
I seemed to know
exactly what was going to
happen before it
happened.
I was so pissed off at
Jane that it had made me
clairvoyant.

"this guy's good,"
I heard somebody
say.

"I can't believe it,"
somebody else
said.

I was right
every time for
the first 3
innings.
I don't know how
many calls I
made,
maybe between
50 or 60 in a
row.

then I got tired of
it all
and decided to
leave.

I walked out to the
parking lot and
the car was
gone.
the bitch had
taken the
car.
I had to get a
cab.

I sat in the back seat
of the cab and
finished the pint of
whiskey.

for some reason
that really
pissed me off.

when I got back to
the apartment Jane was
passed out on the
bed.

I shook her.

"hey, bitch!"

"uh," she said,
"uh . . ."

"listen, I called every
pitch correctly before it
happened!"

"uh . . . ?"

"I called them right
52 times in a
row!"

"uh . . . ?"

her head rolled
over to
one side.
within 5 seconds
she was
snoring.

I went to the
kitchen and got a
beer.
I sat in a chair
and looked at her
snoring on the bed
and drank the
beer.

then I got up and

got a glass of wine
and came back.

I sat in that chair
drinking until it
got dark.

Jane kept snoring and
I kept drinking.

I'd called them right,
I'd called all those
plays
right.

I was young and I was
mean and I was
tough and now I had
something else going
too, something wonderful and
mysterious.

I deserved a younger
woman!
I deserved more
money!
I deserved a better
life!
there was nobody
quite as unique as I
was!

then I gave it up

and went to bed
with all my clothes
on.

burning bright

I read about him in the sports pages,
he's just a kid, he's still in high school,
he's never fought anything but four rounders,
8 four rounders in which he K.O.'d
each one of his 8 opponents
in the first minute of the first
round.

they put him on the card every two weeks
or so
and he waits in his dressing room,
warming up,
then they come in
each time
and tell him the same thing:
the other guy failed to show.

he can't even get anybody to spar with him
down at the gym.

"I'll put him in a six rounder!
I'll put him in a ten rounder!" says his
promoter.

"not enough experience," says his
father, who is his manager.

it's hell when you're too good
to make money.

another young fighter called Van Gogh
found that out.

the death of a hero

I was young when my hero was young
the only difference being that
he quickly became famous
and soon I saw his photograph
in the newspaper
in nightclubs with starlets
and the next thing I knew there was a
war
and he was in uniform
in full garb
but I remembered that in his
books
he had said that he would never ever
go to war.

well, most of us have
heroes
and we don't want them
to be
ordinary,
we want them to be dangerous
and damned well original
and never given over to
any kind or sort of
compromise.

I couldn't understand
how a man could write so
defiantly and clearly
and then proceed to do the
opposite.
I thought that
what you wrote

was from your
soul
and that
such a final
cop-out
by my hero
was impossible.

so I turned on the bastard
and so did the
public—we were not interested
in his books about
army life.

afterwards he went to Malibu and sat on the beach and watched the
waves break on the shore like lies like lies like lies . . .

hooked

28,000 of us sat there on
opening day
one hour before post
with our *Racing Forms*
and our programs and our
newspapers and our coffees
when the announcer said,
"ladies and gentlemen, we regret to
announce that the mutuel clerks
have gone on strike and refuse to
sell tickets so there will be no
racing today. rain checks will be issued at
the gates beginning at
one p.m."
an elderly man in a Hawaiian shirt and black
shoes took out a .45
and blew his left eye out and through the back of his
skull.
everybody felt bad.
"there's nothing to do now," I told my girlfriend,
"but go home and go to bed. we'll race
each other."

the next day I bought a newspaper and looked
to see if it had all really
happened.
it had all really happened.

and when they opened the track again
5 days later

28,000 people sat in the stands again
with their *Racing Forms*
and their programs and their newspapers
and their coffees
one hour before post.

found poems

I know I shouldn't write so many poems
but
it's a form of self-entertainment which
AMAZINGLY
I am paid for.
I live alone in this large house with 2
cats (there were 3, one died)
and at my age it's realistic to assume that
I might also die
one of these a.m. nights
after writing 10 or 12 poems
and that's where the laugh
comes in:
before I bed down I place the new
poems
neatly in the center of my desk so that
when the stink gets bad
and the neighbors complain or
when my girlfriend phones and the phone goes
unanswered

the poems will be found.
not that my death will be tragic or
important

(I will be out of
here)

but the poems themselves will
let them know

(those carping little
critics)

that I was good until the end
or maybe even
better.

runaway inflation

is the light bill
paid?
and the landlord?
they say gasoline
is going to go up
20 cents a gallon
every month
from now on.
soon it will
take a
month's salary
to get a blow job
from an Imperial Highway
hooker.

time to crank grandma's
ass out of the rocker
and *put her* back to work.

all facial tissue and toilet paper
must be used again and again if
possible.

even the birds on the window
sill
must no longer be allowed to
sit there
for free.

this future rolling toward us
paralyzes the wallet and the
brain.

those superior outer space
creatures
can't arrive too soon
for me.
tell them to bring cash.

or maybe they're too smart to want any
part of us?

chances are
the way things are going
only the Imperial Highway hookers
will survive
to finally inherit the
earth.

the significance was obscure

we've been married 30 years,
he told me.

to what do you attribute your marital
success? I asked.

we both roll the toothpaste tube
from the bottom,
he said.

the next morning
before brushing
I rolled the toothpaste tube
from the bottom.

of course, since I live alone,
the significance was
obscure

as it usually
is.

cracking the odds

I've been playing the
horses
for so long
that I have seen
a whole
parade of
jockeys
come and
go
and
women too
and
presidents
but
somehow
for me
the jocks
have become the
markers of my
time.

I've seen them
come in as
bug boys,*
then I've seen
them turn
red hot,
dominate the
meetings—
almost always

*bug boy: an apprentice jock is allowed 5 pounds off the horse's assigned weight until he achieves a certain number of wins or rides a certain number of times, whichever comes first.

getting that
horse's nose
to the wire first
in the photo
finishes.
I've seen them
continue
like that
for a while
and then—
almost at
once—
slow down,
turn
hesitant,
unsure,
and finally
give way
to the next
hot
jock.

in the
arts,
in the field
of entertainment,
in the world
of
business
the same
process
holds
sway

but
the jocks
really
define
the daring
and the
sadness
of the
struggle
for me.

take Johnny
who was
one of the
greatest
front runners
of
our time,
a
real
wire-to-wire
master.
he trains them
now
but isn't very
good
at that.

you can
see him
now
in the tack
room,

tiny
in his chair,
playing cards
with the
Mexican
hot walkers
and
losing
money to
them
day after
day.

"hey, Johnny,
you wanna
play cards,
man?"

jocks like Johnny
define the
tragedy of life
for me
more than does
the
passing of
Marco Polo,
Picasso
or
Henry the
8th.

jocks like Johnny
define life's struggle

for me,
so small and
brave.

while Kant
lies stiff in
his
grave
and Mozart
turns to dust

Johnny
flips
down a
card

and
finally
wins
a
hand.

working through it all

the bravery of some is close to fear
and the fear of some is close to
bravery
and I admire a brave man more than a fearful
man,
and sometimes I am one or the other
and often I am neither.

that's when I'm best: neither brave nor
fearful

just cracking nuts in my warm
alcove

as flowers strain to grow
as music strives to please

as the ladies love
others.

giving thanks

I have to admire
that most abused of the human
species:
the white American
middle-class
male.

as a writer
I have been criticized for
writing unkindly of
females;
other writers have been
criticized
for writing unkindly of
Blacks,
Orientals,
homosexuals,
lesbians,
Amerindians,
the aged,
the unborn
the newly
born
the lame
or the Chicanos
the Jews
the French
the Italians
the Greeks
the English
or the
whatevers.

actually,
making mild minor
sport of
or criticizing
almost any minority
group
has ruined the
careers of not only
writers but
politicians
sports commentators,
and people in
entertainment.

it is a touchy age.
everybody is on the
defensive.
you must not
speak unkindly about
us,
they say,
or
we will finish
you
off!

now for a writer,
this is grade-a
hell.
a good writer
must simply let
it all go,
regardless.

if I find a Black
or a woman
or a dog
or a cripple
or a tree
or a child
or an Oriental
individually
obnoxious
I think it is my
duty to describe
them as
such.

I often describe myself
as obnoxious,
for example.

I demand that all territories
be open for
criticism!

I will not
be guilty of
treading
heavily
on the truth!

even so,
I still give everlasting
thanks
to the white American
middle-class

male
who can still be trashed and
insulted and
demeaned again and
again
and no one ever protests,
and he never protests,
he just doesn't give a
damn.

but, oh, says the
politically correct
chorus,
they're just too satisfied
with their mundane
existence!

yes, some of them
are,
but not all of them.
some of them are
just as heroic
as homosexuals
and lesbians
and feminists,
and Blacks,
and all the etceteras;
and in some cases,
even more
so.
but our white American
middle-class male

never protests
when I find *him*
out of
order.

but, says the
politically correct chorus,
that's because
he's running the
show!

maybe,
maybe not.

all I know is
that as a writer
he's a good and fair
and uncomplaining
target
for me.
I can abuse him
and punch
him,
I can lay him
low in the
poem,
I can abuse him
in stories, novels and
screenplays,
and he'll take it all
without a
whimper.

in our very restrictive
overprotective
society
it's great for a writer
to have one such wide-open
playground to play
around
in.

so again here's to
the white American middle-class
male,
the butt of
all the jokes,
the clown,
the brute,
the watcher of tv,
the dog,
the drinker of beer,
the sexist pig,
the bumbling husband,
the fat-bellied
dim-witted
nincompoop
who will take every
possible abuse
and say
nothing,
he'll just
light a fresh
cigar,
shift uncomfortably in his

chair and try to
smile.

here's to this
forgotten
hero!

now, go
ahead,
hate
me.

Los Angeles

there is an old saying:
that those whom the gods wish to
destroy,
they first make
angry.

driving the freeways
each day
it appears to me
that
the gods are getting
ready
to
destroy the entire
City
of
Angels.

2,294

spoiled woman
washing your panties
in suds and cold water

your eyes are angry
as they watch me
and the world

you feel that you've wasted
your years
and yourself

it didn't work
for me
either

but isn't there always
one good thing
to look back on?

think of
how many cups of coffee we
drank together.

why do you write so many poems about death?

Shakespeare's dead.

photo of dead Hemingway
downstairs in the hall:
For Whom the Bell Tolls.

Pascal.
Hitler.
Sammy Davis Jr.
Marconi.

the little old lady next door who watered her
geraniums.

the hunting dogs of the mad Count
Dracula.

almost all the Tarzans.

and Jane.

my first
wife
and
Primo Carnera.

and you're going to die too,
old man, you and your white
legs,
you and your pose,
devil-may-care,
playing it tough

like you know it
all.

smoking and typing
you look down, you're in your
shorts
and on your leg a spot of
blood.
what?
something drips.
it's your
nose.
some of it has dripped
onto your shirt.

Christ, your wife will be
pissed.

evidence

whores and great poets should
avoid one another:
their professions are dangerously
similar:
from the Roman Empire to our
Atomic Age
there have been about an equal
number of whores and
poets
with the authorities continually
trying to outlaw
the former
and ignore the latter
—which tells you
how dangerous
poetry
really
is.

part 3

the problem with
c
o
n
c
r
e
t
poetry
i
s
the
s
a
m
as the

problem with
c
o
n
c
r
e
t
people

a wise ass

that's what I was on campus, some of the professors, I'm sure,
feared me or at least preferred that I not be in their
class.
I had a scarred and lean countenance and I slouched
in my seat
hungover and dangerous.
I refused to buy the assigned books or study.
I was insolent, cool and crazy and I drank and fought every night.
my parents supported me out of fear.
I was the meanest 18-year-old son of a bitch in the
world.
I would leap up in class and make incoherent
speeches challenging whatever the professor had just
said.
I was a pain in the ass and I thought I was tough but I was afraid to
go out for the football team or ask a girl for a
date.
I guess I was crazy.
all I read was Nietzsche and Schopenhauer.
I was taking journalism and art classes and
when they asked us for one writing assignment a
week, I wrote seven.
some said I was a genius.
I felt like a genius or I felt like I thought a genius
should feel.
one day I got in a fight after art class with the
200-pound fullback of the football team.
we fought for 30 minutes on the campus
lawn.
unfortunately nobody stopped us.
I finally won although I never expected to.
I kept waiting to lose and it didn't happen.
then I began to get popular and I couldn't take that so

I pretended to be a born-again Nazi.
then I got a lot of freaky guys full of hate trailing
after me so
I told them to fuck off and I became the school
recluse.
I don't know, after two years on campus I didn't
want it anymore so
I quit and got a job in the railroad yards as a
laborer.
I rented a small room downtown and roamed the
streets at night.
some genius I was, some god-damned
genius!
I made several trips to the *Herald-Examiner* and the
L.A. Times and told them I wanted to become a
reporter.
I never made it past the receptionist's desk.
"fill out these forms," they said.
I shoved them back.
they didn't know I was a genius.

one night in a bar I got in a fight with a little
guy, he must have weighed only 130 pounds.
he whipped my ass.
the next night I tested him once more.
he whipped my ass all over again.

a week later I took a bus to New Orleans.
somewhere along the way I bought a book by
a famous guy called
Hemingway.
I couldn't read it.
the fucking guy couldn't write!

I tossed the book out the window.
a girl on the bus kept staring at me.
she turned in her seat and made a
sketch of my face.
she wrote her address on
the back of the sketch and
got off at Fort Worth.
I went on to Dallas, got off, caught a shave,
showered at the "Y,"
took a bus back to Fort Worth and found her.
I sat in the front room with her while her mother
sat in the bedroom.
we talked a long time, it was great, she was beautiful.
then she held my hand and
started talking about God and I got the
fuck out of there.

I took another bus to New Orleans.
I had a portable typewriter with me.
that's all that I needed
to prove I was a genius.
that, and another 35
years.

the dressmaker

my first wife made her own dresses
which I thought was nice.
I'd often see her bent over her
sewing machine
putting together a new dress.
we were both working and I thought
it was great that she found the time
to create her own
wardrobe.

then one evening I came home and
she was crying.
she told me that some guy at work
had told her that she had bad
taste in her wearing
apparel.
he had said she looked
"tacky."

"do you think I dress tacky?"
she asked.
"of course not.
who is this guy?
I'll beat hell out of him!"

"you can't, he's my boss."

she cried some more that
evening.
I tried to reassure her and she
finally stopped.

but after that, she purchased
all her dresses.
I thought that
they didn't look nearly as good on her
but she told me that the fellow at work
had praised her new
clothes.

well, as long as she stopped
crying
I was satisfied.

then one day she asked me, "which do
you like best, my old dresses or
the new ones?"

"you look good either way," I
answered.

"yes, but which do you *prefer*?
the old dresses or the new ones?"

"the old ones," I told her.

then she began crying again
and wouldn't stop.

there were similar problems with other
aspects of our
marriage.

when she divorced me she was still
wearing only the store-bought
dresses

but she took the sewing machine
with her
and a suitcase filled with dresses
of the old
kind.

lunch in Beverly Hills

it's a shame, it's a damned shame,
sitting here at this table
spread with a clean white tablecloth,
on a veranda overlooking Beverly Blvd.
a light lunch, you might even say a
business lunch, your lawyer has
collected some money due you from
a movie producer.
your bright energetic lady
lawyer, her assistant and my wife,
we eat and drink wine, and then order coffee and talk
mostly about the impending war
as at all the tables around us
there is more talk about the im-
pending war (although at the table just
behind us some men laugh loudly
so they must be talking about
something else).

I feel very strange, very odd
that we are sitting at this table
spread with an immaculate white
tablecloth with all the successful
people sitting here with us
with the war about to start
tomorrow
or next week
as we sit over wine and coffee
on a beautiful, clear day in
Beverly Hills.

and although I am guilty of nothing,
I feel guilty nonetheless.

I think that I would feel better about every
thing if I was sitting instead in a cheap room
with flies crawling my wine
cup.
not pleasant, of course, but at least it's war of
another kind.

but I am in Beverly Hills and that is
all that there is to
it.

I reach for my gold card as I
twist in my chair and
ask the waiter for the
bill.

she was really mad

I love you, she said,
and spit in a bowl of
jello
put it in the
refrigerator
and said,
you can eat that later
for dinner!

then she was gone
like a whirlwind
out the door
in a rush of angry
skirt.

a tree, a road, a toad

a table of 7, all
laughing loudly, again and again,
almost deafening,
but there is no joy in their
laughter, it seems machine
made.
the pretense and falsity
poison the air.
the other diners seem not to
notice.
I am asphyxiated by the laughter,
my gut, my mind, my very meaning
gag on it.
I dream of taking a gun, of
walking over to the table
and blowing their heads off,
one by one.
of course, this would make me
far more guilty than they
are.
still, I have the thought and
then I realize that I expect too
much.
I should have long ago
realized that this is the way
it is:
that everywhere there are tables of 2,
3, 7, 10 or more
where people
laugh meaninglessly and
without joy,
laugh inanely without
real feeling,

and that this is an inevitable part
of all that,
like a tree, a road, a toad.

I order another drink and
decide not to kill them, even
in my imagination.

I decide, instead, that I am a
very lucky man:
the table is twenty feet away.
I could be *at* that table, sitting there
with them,
close to their mouths,
close to their eyes and their ears
and their hands,
actually *listening* to the conversation
which is causing their joyless
laughter.
I have been in many such situations before
and it has been one bloody cross,
indeed.

so, I settle for my good fortune
but can't help but wonder
if there is any place left in the world
with a table of 7 where
there are genuine feelings,
where there is
great and real laughter.
I hope so.
I have to hope so.

in one ear and out the other

my father had memorized many sayings that he liked to
repeat over and over:
"if you can't succeed, suck eggs!"
"my country, right or wrong!"
"early to bed and early to rise makes a man healthy,
wealthy and wise!"

my mother just smiled as he mouthed these
pearls of wisdom.
me?
I thought, this man is a fool.

"any man who wants a job can get one!" was one
of his favorites during the Depression years.

almost everything he said was stupid.
he called my mother "mama."
"mama, we gotta move out of this neighborhood!"
"why, daddy?"
"because I saw one, mama!"
"one what, daddy?"
"a nigger . . ."

another one of his favorites was:
"eenie, meanie, miney, mo, catch a nigger by the
toe, if he hollers make him pay, 50 dollars every
day!"

he never voiced these aphorisms while sitting down
but always while marching smartly about the
house.
"God helps those who help themselves!"

"you listen to your father, Henry," my mother would
tell me.
that poor woman, she meant it.

"don't do as I do," he'd shout, "but do as I
say!"
I ended up doing neither.

and the day I looked down at him in his
coffin
I almost expected him to say something
but he didn't so I spoke up for
him:
"dead men tell no more tales."

thank Christ, I had heard enough.

then
they closed the lid and my uncle Jack and
I went out for hamburgers and fries.

we sat there with the food in front of us.

"your father was a good man," Uncle Jack
said.

"Jack," I replied, "good for what?"

excuses

once again
I hear of somebody who is going to
settle down and
do their work,
painting or writing or whatever,
as soon as they get a better light
installed,
or as soon as they move to a new
city,
or as soon as they come back from the trip they
have been planning,
or as soon as . . .

it's simple: they just don't want
to do it,
or they can't do it,
otherwise they'd feel a burning
itch from hell
they could not ignore
and "soon"
would turn quickly into
"now."

bygone days

once upon a time men used to wait in
the front room, smoking cigars, drinking brandy
and discussing the important things, the manly
things, as the ladies worked in the kitchen
preparing dinner while we enjoyed the
aroma of spices, the smell of
cooking meat and our conversation.

always, there was plenty of brandy and more serious talk.

we had come through some very difficult times
the wars and what-not and
now we were in charge, invincible and very male: our
expectations, our dress, our manner,
we were as lions resting comfortably
in our homes as the feast was
prepared.

it was our just due. no questions asked.

at mealtime we would fill ourselves,
offering up appreciative grunts,
nodding affirmatives to our ladies; we were well fed and
well pleased.

then followed the removal of the main course and on to the
dessert and the coffee.

that done, the ladies would remove the empty
plates and we would relax awhile over our coffee
as the ladies began washing the dishes in the
kitchen.

"let's go back to the front room," the host would finally
say.

there we would switch from brandy to whiskey or scotch.
sobered by the meal we lighted fine Cuban
cigars as the sound of running water and the clanking of
plates emanated from the kitchen.

yes, the world was exactly as we wanted it to be

until female liberation began and now we are often
found in the kitchen, washing the dishes, and sometimes we even
        have to
cook the meal, too.

the ladies now go cocktailing around 2:30 p.m.,
chatting, gossiping, they get giddy, giggle, and often
are intoxicated. sometimes they get into tearful
arguments.

the kitchen is forgotten; the ladies are
liberated; they chain-smoke and wear pantsuits instead of
dresses; they curse simply as a matter of course;
they toss around words like "fuck" and "shit" and
they are particularly fond of shouting "piss off!"
they spill drinks on themselves, laugh hysterically.

the men are uncomfortable and exchange little side
glances; they say nothing, just as the women used to
do.

the men have given up smoking, and drink sparingly:
they are now the "designated drivers."

the ladies discuss everything: politics, world
affairs, philosophy, art and sundry other matters.

once in a while one of the men will speak out. it will
usually be something about sports, like, "I think the Yankees need
a new center fielder."

"what?" one of the other men will say. "I didn't hear you."

the ladies are laughing, talking loudly, cursing, smoking,
pouring fresh drinks . . .

"what?"

"I said, 'I think the Yankees need a new center fielder.'"

"oh yes, I think you're right."

then the men will fall back into a profound silence.

they are waiting for night to fall.

in a lady's bedroom

trying to write a poem
in a lady's bedroom
(onions on my breath)
while she cuts a dress
out of freshly bought
material.

I suppose, as material,
I'm not so fresh,
especially with onions
on my breath.

well, let's see—
there's a lady in Echo Park,
one in Pasadena, one
in Sacramento, one on
Harvard Ave.
perhaps one of them would be more interested
in me
than in a dress (for a while,
anyhow).

meanwhile I sit in this
lady's bedroom
by a hot window
while she sits at her
sewing machine.

here, she said, here's a
paper and pen,
write something.

all right, I'll be kind:
some ladies fuck like mink
and dance like nymphs
and some create
nice dresses and lonely poets
on hot July
afternoons.

model friend

Wentworth worked as a model.
he even got paid for it and he didn't
look any different from
the rest of us.

"put on your cap for Hank. show
him how you posed as a sea
captain," said Clara.

Clara was his woman.
I was with Jane.

we were drinking in their apartment,
a very nice place.
we lived in a tiny room
just a few blocks away and were far
behind in the rent.

we had brought along our own wine
and they were drinking it.
I was 40 pounds underweight
barely alive and
going crazy.

Wentworth got his cap and
put it on.
it was blue and flopped just
right.
he stood in front of a full-
length mirror and smiled.

I was being sued in the aftermath
of a driving accident

had ulcers
and every time I drank whiskey I
spit up blood.

"Wentworth," I told him, "you look
dashing."

why don't they give us something to
eat? I thought. can't they see that
we're starving?

Wentworth turned from the mirror
and looked at me. "modeling is a
good show. what do you do?"

"Hank's a writer," Jane said.

Jane was a good girl: she answered all the
questions for me.

"oh," said Clara, "how fascinating!
how's it going?"

"things are a little slow," I
said.

Wentworth sat down and poured himself
another drink.

"wanna arm wrestle?" he asked me.

"o.k.," I said, "I'll try you."

we bellied up to the table, came to
grips, nodded, and he slammed my arm
on the table
like a marsh reed.

"well," I said, "you were best that
time."

"wanna try another?"

"not right away."

"maybe I can get you into
modeling?"

"what as?"

"or into a secretarial position.
how many words can you type a minute?"

"I'm into longhand right now."

"what do you write about?"

"death."

"death? nobody wants to read about
that."

"I think you're right."

the girls were talking to each other.
then Clara got up and went to the

bedroom.
she was there awhile.
then she came out with a new hat
on.
she stood,
smiling.

"oh, Clara," said Jane, "it's
lovely!"

"women don't wear hats anymore," said
Clara, "but I just *love* hats!"

"you *should,* you look so *dear!*"

so there was Wentworth in his blue sea
captain's cap and there was Clara in her new
purple foxglove.

"wanna try another arm wrestle?" asked
Wentworth. "the best two out of
three?"

"just pour me a drink."

"oh, sorry . . ."

the evening continued and we got to be good
friends, I suppose.
we sang some songs, sea songs among them,
and Wentworth gave me a cigar.
I was proud of Jane.
she had a great little figure, just

right.
even when we didn't eat for days I was
the only one who lost weight
which sometimes gave me the idea that
she might be eating someplace else while I
practiced my new longhand prose style.
but it didn't matter: she deserved the
food.

meanwhile
I begged off the arm wrestling and we
kept drinking my wine.
when it was gone
the evening was over.

I remember standing in their doorway
hugging him and her
saying
goodbye, yes, yes, it was a great
evening.

and then the door closed and
there was the empty street.
as we walked back to our
room Jane said, "look at that
moon! isn't that moon
wonderful?"
I couldn't say it was so I
didn't answer.

then we were standing in the hall of our
roominghouse.

I took out the key
and stuck it in the door and it snapped in
half and the door wouldn't open and the key
wouldn't come back out so I gave the door what
shoulder I had and it split open and
as it did some guy down the hall hollered,
"HEY, YOU GOD-DAMNED DRUNKS, I GOT A
GOOD MIND TO SEND YOU DOWN THE RIVER IN A
SACK OF SHIT!"

it sounded like mr. big mouth lived in
room 8.

I walked down to room 8 and
knocked. "come on out," I said. "I've got
something for you."

there wasn't any answer.

Jane was at my side. "you've got the
wrong door."

"I've got the right door," I told her.
I BANGED on the son of a bitch.

"COME ON OUT, FUCKER! I'LL KILL YOU!"

"it was room 9," said Jane.
"you got the wrong door."

I walked down to 9 and BANGED again. "COME ON
OUT, FUCKER, AND I'LL KILL YOU!"

"if you don't go away," I heard a voice say
from behind the door, "I'm going to call the
police!"

"you chickenshit scum," I said.

I walked back to our room and Jane
followed me.
she closed the door and I sat down
on the edge of the bed and pulled off
my shoes and stockings.

"your buddy in the sailor cap," I
told her, "he gets on my
nerves."

the invitation

listen, Chinaski, we've always LOVED your work, we've got all your books, especially the dirty ones, you just really get the word down and we love you, I love you, and I just busted up with my old man, he liked your stuff too, he was the one who introduced me to your shit and now I'm living with a guy in his pick-up truck who makes his living at swap meets, he hates your writing but I hated it too when I first read it, anyhow the rest of us (and we're some GANG) we've got this idea, we're kind of Funk City, you know, and we thought we'd throw a party in CELEBRATION OF YOU, we don't bow down to too many pricks but your stuff just tears us up, SO—we got together and scrounged up a few chips (that's MONEY, HONEY) and we'll meet you at the airport, we got this great orange VW for one and then there's Ricky's pick-up, so there's TRANSPORTATION, and there's a *good* gang here, plenty of beer and you see we want to CELEBRATE YOU in the way you deserve and even tho you're an ugly fuck we can probably (?) line you up with something young and tender. maybe we can also fix you up a reading at the local bar, plenty of cowboys and x-cons who understand where you're coming from, you gotta be the greatest writer since Kerouac and so here it is—our invitation—in honor of ya, come on up and if nobody will lay you my pussy ain't too dry, ain't too bad, I'm 22 and last month I went to the Naropa Institute over in Colorado, to their last fucking function, and I asked, "WHERE'S CHINASKI?" and they acted like they never heard the name, that bunch could make the Sphinx puke, really, so listen, let us know soon!!!!

     love,
       MOONCHILD

PS:
832-4170 (I use the phone at the pharmacy, ask for Larry and tell him ya got a message for the KEEPER OF THE STARS AND BARS, he'll know who you mean!)

Hollywood hustle

the first one came up to me while I was
eating in the Italian cafe
and he said,
"pardon me, sir, may I read the Home Section
of your newspaper?"
"no," I said, "you may not."

I finished eating and went outside and
another guy stopped me at the corner:
"hey, Jack, can you use a
watch?"
he opened his hand and in his
palm was a
wristwatch. "can't use it,"
I said.

I walked across the street and down a
block and another guy stopped
me. he was carrying 2
pool sticks.
"listen," he said, "I need 50 cents more
to get a meal. and by the way, can I
sell you a pool stick?"

I shook my head,
gave him a quarter and walked
on.

a man shouldn't say "no" all night
long and I just can't shoot a
decent game of
pool.

Buddha Chinaski says

sometimes
you have to take
a step or
two
back,
re-
treat

take
a month
off

don't
do anything
don't
want to
do anything

peace is
paramount
pace is
paramount

whatever
you want
you aren't going to
get
it by
trying too
hard.

take
ten years
off

you'll
be
stronger

take
twenty years
off

you'll
be much
stronger.

there's nothing to
win
anyhow

and
remember
the second best thing in
the world
is
a good night's
sleep

and
the best:
a gentle
death.

meanwhile
pay your gas
bill
if you can
and
stay out of
arguments with the
wife.

like Lazarus

the unknown time and place of
your death is a
mystery, isn't it?
also the manner of your
death?
you can go while tying a
shoelace
or you can go with a knife
in your belly.

you can go in fear,
you can go in peace,
you can go without being aware
of either.

in L.A. County General Hospital
my ward was next to the
operating room.
I was a poor sleeper
and I was often awake
between 3 and 6 a.m.
and that was when they
wheeled the bodies
out,
bodies covered
with a sheet,
and the doors would swing open
and the heads would
come out first,
then the remainder of
the body
followed,

rolled along by the
white-clad
orderly.

I always counted the
bodies.
one, two, three,
four every blessed
night.

no need for me to
count sheep,
I had something better.

one night they broke
the record (at least
during my sojourn),
they got up to
8.

I waited and waited
for #9
but he/she never
came.

the sun finally came up
however
and the bedpans
were rattled
and the nurses
made grim jokes
and complained of their

domestic
problems.

our ward was a
special ward
where they put the
desperate cases,
we were all
teetering on the
edge
and some of us
finally
went
over,
but the goings
(at least during my
sojourn)
weren't bloody,
ugly or even
dramatic.
there was even
a tinge of boredom
about it
all.

"Mr. Williams, Mr. Williams . . .
here's your breakfast!
Mr. Williams?
Mr. Williams?
oh, he's
gone . . ."

there was never an
empty bed
for long.
they changed the
sheets and Williams was
replaced by Miss Jones and when
Jones went she was
replaced by
Mr. Wong.

and the sun came
up blazing
in the mornings
just to taunt us
and there was much
time to waste.
we were too far gone to speak
to one another and
the only sounds were
wheezing and
occasional bits of
coughing or
groaning
and every now and then
a weak and pitiable voice
mewing
"nurse . . . nurse . . ."

I left that place, that palace
of death, without looking
back.
I went down the aisle

between the beds
and
then down many
steps
(I didn't count
them)
and out the front
entrance into the
street.

I phoned the cab
from a nearby
bar.
the cab took me over
the bridge,
over the invisible
L.A. River
and we went back
to my part of
town.
it was a crazy feeling
finally
being
out.

I paid the cabby and
went up the
walk.
I still had my key,
I put it in the front door
and opened
it.

the room was on the
second floor,
up a steep
stairway.

the dog met me halfway
up.
he was a big one,
he leaped at me
joyously,
his tail whipping like a
snake on
fire.
I was still weak and
he almost pushed me
over.

I walked on up the
stairway and down the long hall
and into the small
room.

she was sitting on the
couch, smoking a
cigarette and
reading a
magazine.

startled,
she looked
up.

"Jesus, why didn't you
tell me?"
she asked.

"what's there to
tell?
is there any
beer?"

she got up, walked quickly
into the kitchen
with an uneasy smile,
looking back at me
over her
shoulder.

soft and fat like summer roses

Rex was a two-fisted man
who drank like a fish
and looked like a purple anemone.
he married three others
before he found the right one.
they fought over cheap gin
were friendless
and satisfied
and frightened the landlord.
then she began to holler plenty
and he would listen dully,
then leap up red with choice words
until she began again.
it was a good life,
soft and fat like summer roses.

good bedmates
they were
until he got hurt at work, near
fatally, it seemed,
and he stayed in bed then
smiling it off
while she got a job as a waitress
in a cheap café
where the lads were rather rough,
sometimes drunk, slapping her rear while
Rex drank gin in bed while
she walked about, saying nothing,
thinking about a Greek who came in
    mornings,
touched her hand, quietly said "eggs,
eggs again."

Rex continued to drink gin in bed
and one night she didn't come back.
nor the next. nor the next.
and with a lurch, he got out of bed
and walked holding to walls
around and around and around
and fell, clutching the carpet,
saying, "o, Christ! o, Christ!"

the Greek was very different,
he didn't drink at all and
said he believed in God,
he loved diffidently, like a butterfly,
and he had a new refrigerator.

Rex was sitting in bed with the gin
one dark night
when she returned, saying nothing.

"bitch! cheap bitch!" he said as
she sat down on the bed, fully dressed,
and looked pleased to see him.
later he stood upright on the floor,
    smiling and himself again, and
said, "I'm going back to work tomorrow
    morning.
and you, you stay out of that goddamn café!"

in transit

the French border guard had a black waxed
mustache and an ivory face with pimples
for eyes.
he stank of perfume and his uniform
was wrinkled but his boots were
new and shiny: the overhead
lights reflected in them and made
me dizzy.
he was frosty, he was filled with a
strange cold rage.

it was only 15 degrees outside
but in that building
with too much heating and all the hot
lights
it must have been
110.

the heat
only maddened the
guard.
little drops of sweat ran down his nose
and dripped off.
he looked dangerous.

"PASSPORT!" he screamed.

I handed it over, smiling blandly at him.

he poked at the photo.

"IS THIS YOU?"

"yes, sir."

"YOU LOOK YOUNGER THAN THIS
PHOTOGRAPH!"

"I was ill when the photo was
taken . . ."

"ILL? WHAT WAS IT?"

"the flu . . ."

"THE FLU?"

I didn't reply.

he opened my suitcase and
began to take the contents
out.
he flung them all about, then
stopped.

"WHAT ARE THESE
PAPERS?"

"paintings . . ."

"WHOSE?"

"I painted them."

he glared at me, his wax mustache
quivering.
then,

"ALL RIGHT. YOU CAN GO
THROUGH!"

I went to work gathering up my
things.

next in line was a voluptuous
young lady.
the guard snatched her
passport, looked at it, then smiled
at her.

I had my suitcase put together
and was leaving
when I heard him:

"he said he was a painter!"

then I was out of there and soon
I was out of the building
and into the 15
degrees
and it was so fine and lovely
out there, truly
refreshing.

"dear Mr. Chinaski"

I have tried your publisher with my
work.
they didn't understand my poems
and they say their schedule is
filled for now,
so I thought maybe you should read
my manuscript
and then talk to them.
I've also enclosed an envelope for your
response.
I've long been an admirer of your
work,
and I don't want to kiss your ass,
but I consider you one of our
greatest living writers,
so if you would just look over the poems
enclosed, I'll be forever in
your debt.

one of the greatest living writers
read them,
trashed them, including the stamped
and addressed
return envelope.

what a helpless soft son of a bitch!

the way he wrote he
was.

silverfish

"SILVERFISH!" my father would
holler and my mother would come
running with the special can
of spray.

my father was always finding
silverfish.
it seemed to go on for days
and years on
end:
"SILVERFISH!"

I saw a silverfish
now and then
but I never said
anything.

mostly they liked to hang
around the bathtub
or in dark wet
places.

they hardly seemed a
threat
to me.

but my father's hysterical excitement
upon finding a
silverfish
never
abated.

well, it did after my
mother's death
because my father had nobody
to holler at.

then my father died
and in his casket he looked
just like—
you know—
a big one.

but I didn't holler
anything.

the popularity kid

they are good fellows all, in one way or another,
but they all seem to find you on the same day at
the racetrack, especially when your mood isn't one of
the best.
the first one, you don't remember his name,
he pushes his face real close
and starts talking fast and loud but the meaning
of what he says passes right over your head.
after a bit you
break away from him somehow and maybe there's 15
minutes' peace, then a mutuel clerk catches your
eye, waves you over, he's one big smile, grabs
your hand and pumps it, he's asking about some-
body you both know but it's really about nothing
at all. "have you seen Mike
lately?"
"no, I haven't."
luckily, somebody behind me wants to buy a
ticket and I quickly move away.

a race passes and I am walking along when another
poor soul jumps me, he's all smiles too and he pumps
my hand but doesn't say anything, he just stares,
smiling, smiling.
he's in the horse business and I ask him something
about his horses and when I get the answer
I say, "great!" then spin on my heel and move
off.

just before the last race I am approached by two
complete strangers.
now, I am going to have to say something ugly.
I have absolutely no interest in any of these people

and never would approach them myself.
why do they feel a need for me?
is it cordiality? fear? respect? boredom?

and it's not only the racetrack, it's wherever I
go.
say, in my supermarket, the manager will rush toward
me, his arms widespread.
there is this sushi place, when I enter, the owner will
greet me and bow low.
he does not do this for his other customers.
at a Mexican restaurant I frequent, the owner
always rushes over, slides into my booth, puts an arm
about me and says, "it's good to see you!"
at this Chinese place, the waitresses gather around
my table, chatter, make jokes and expound
little Oriental philosophies.
it also happens to me in gas stations, etc.
I never make the first overture, I always try to keep a low
profile but it doesn't seem to help.

what is it?
I don't find myself interesting.
it must be pity, I must look woeful,
at death's door.
but then, thinking back, all this began when I was
about 16 years old, people began trailing me, wanting
to be friends, attaching themselves to me.
granted, many of them were mentally defective, but not
all of them.
it was back then when I first began evading
people, hiding from them, finding excuses to
discard them as friends, and it has gone on ever since.

I'm a god-damned magnet to the human herd
and I don't like it and I don't want it and it won't
stop.
I'm just going to have to die to get away and even that
might not work:
the ghouls will come running toward me, arms outstretched,
saying, "hey, Chinaski, we've been waiting for you!
we wanna drink beer with you and talk!
just talk and drink beer!
now we can hang out with you
forever, baby, FOREVER!"

death and white glue

the tiny summer creatures are flying
all around here now and
I have nothing to
smoke.

now
all around here
tiny summer creatures fly.
I usually blow smoke at them
and at the lamp bulb
and watch the smoke curl in the air
and sometimes think of things
like
death and white glue.
the summer creatures bite at night
when I am asleep
and in the morning I have bumps on my
body
which are delightful to
scratch.

my love is upstairs watching a comedy on
tv.
down here I am drinking wine
Liebfraumilch
and my love considers this a
betrayal of our love, but
you and I know what a betrayal of love really
is.

meanwhile
I crush some of the tiny summer creatures
some find the white glue

but I leave a few of them
so that I am able to scratch myself in the
morning.

the summer creatures are so strange
I feel that they know me—
one falls into my glass of
Liebfraumilch
I watch him flick and kick about
and then I
drink him down.

I hope that comedy is good
upstairs. I have my own show going on down
here.

fun times: 1930

Harold was always scared.
he was easy.
we had a good time with
Harold.

we'd pretend to hang him 2 or 3 times
a week.

we had a rope and we'd
corner him on the back porch
of Mrs. Keller's place.
there was a heavy
rafter.
we'd put the rope around
his neck.

"this time we're gonna do
it, Harold, we're tired of
fucking around.
this time we're *really* going
to hang you!"

"oh, no! *please!*"

he would cry silently, the
tears rolling down his stupid
freckled face.

"stop your damned blubbering!
now, if you don't want to die either you
got to drink piss or eat shit!
which do you want?"

Harold would just keep crying.

"which do you want? answer or
we'll hang you now!"

"piss," he would always say.

then we'd piss on him, all over
his shoes and his pants, while
laughing.

then
when his family finally moved out of
the neighborhood we set fire to
Mrs. Gorman's chicken coop.

my bully

he was big and he was always after me
down at the loading dock.
"I'm gonna kick your ass," he told me.
"listen, Jimmy, there are 50 guys out
here, why don't you kick somebody
else's ass?"
"no," he said, "I'm gonna kick *your*
ass."
well, I couldn't blame him.
there was something about me, a
lot of guys wanted to kick my ass, I'd
had that problem for years.
maybe I looked easy, maybe it was
because I was good-natured, liked to
clown around.
anyhow, I had a problem and it was
Jimmy, all 230 pounds of him.

it was midweek and we were
sitting around eating lunch out of our
brown bags
when Jimmy reached and
grabbed my sandwich.
"what the fuck is this?" he asked.
he took the sandwich in his
fist and crushed it into a
round ball.
then he rolled it on the ground.
"well, hell," I said, "I'm on a diet,
anyhow."
"a diet, huh?" said Jimmy.
he held up a big right hand and

doubled it up.
"maybe you'd like to eat my
fist?"
"hey, Jimmy baby, I'm no
cannibal."
"JUST SHUT UP!" he screamed.
I
shut up.

I don't know, he just kept after me
with his threats and somehow I
didn't feel like I deserved any of
it.

then management moved me to a
small office on the dock.
it was Sunday.
there was nothing to do, I just
answered the phone and tried to
look wise.

Jimmy was working that
Sunday.
he stood there glaring at me through
the glass partition.
then he began coming toward me.
I was feeling depressed, I had just
split with my shackjob.

Jimmy walked up.
"come on out of there, I'm going to beat
the shit out of you!" he said.

"all right, Jimmy," I said.
I came out and moved toward him, thinking,
I better get in a few shots fast because that's
all I've got time for.
he backed off a little and I caught him on
the nose with the first right.
his nose moved back into his head and spurted
red.
I'm dead now, I thought, and my left caught him
on the ear.
I put a right to his belly and it was soft, my fist
seemed to sink in half a foot.
Jimmy fell to the ground and held his face and
began sobbing like a
girl.

I looked around at the guys.
"what the fuck," I said, "this guy is a fake."

"Jesus," somebody said.

we all drifted away.
I went back to the office, sat down.
after a while Jimmy got up, walked down
to the end of the loading dock, jumped off, and disappeared
into the alley.

we never saw him again.

I never really understood what it all meant.

and nobody ever talked about him
to me again.
it was like it never
happened.

fellow runs a bookstore
I go in there and sign my books for
    him
and he always forces a book on me
something about the rough-and-tumble
    life
but these books are written by
newspaper
    columnists
professors, born-into-wealthers,
    etc.
and these have seen about as much real
    low life
as a parish priest;
    their lives
have been about as adventuresome as
dusting a library
    shelf
and none of them has ever missed a
    meal.
these books are well written,
sometimes clever
just a touch
    daring
but there is an overriding sense
of comfort
in the writing and in the
    life.
the books fall from my
    hand.
this bookstore fellow is
going to have to think
of some other means of

        rewarding
me for
        signing my books
because reading this nicely
printed
        crap
only reminds me
once again
that I am competing only
against
        myself.

the singers

it was a Sunday night. I found a booth,
ordered a beer and dinner, and waited.
there were two musicians, a
man with a guitar and a woman who sang
with the man as he played.
they went from table to table, from booth to
booth, serenading the customers who were
mostly families with children.
the songs were popular melodies that I had
heard many times before and despised.
it was tired stuff, worn and played to death.
my dinner was slow in arriving and I ordered
another beer.
the singers finished at a table, then turned and
approached me.
I raised my hands, waved them off, said,
"no, no, no!"
they walked past to the booth behind me and
began.
they had wanted to share their
mediocre music with me
but I had warded them off.
I felt quite proud of my quick decision
to do so.

my dinner arrived and I ate in peace.

ten years ago, maybe even five, I would
have allowed the singers to descend on
me, but no longer.

often it takes a lifetime to learn how to
react to certain critical situations.

it's worth waiting for the arrival of maturity
and confidence.
try it sometime and see how delightful it
is to feel powerful and
alive.

the march

whenever I hear the *March to the
Gallows*
playing on the radio
I think of her
in that blue milkmaid's dress
that showed off her
figure
there in Santa Fe.
it was raining
the *March* was playing
the rain was pouring down
there were even candles
burning!
it was a large but
comfortable
house
and I told her what she
was doing to
me,
how much I
wanted her,
what a miracle it
was.
I was so poor and so
ugly
and there I was
with
her!
but I was also a
fool
and I loved my
wine

and I foolishly played the
foolish drunk as
the *March* played
on and on
in that warm room,
it would end, then
play once
again

I looked over
and there she was
on the couch,
absolutely
naked,
milk-
white.

an astonishing
frightening
and riveting
sight

"I'll be right there,"
I said, "just one more
drink."

I never made it
there.

she drove me to the
airport the
next day.

some months passed
and then there was a
letter from
her.

you looked so sad
on that drive to the airport.
I've thought of you often.
I bought a new car,
bright red, it's silly
but I can't think of the
name, you know, who
made it. it's raining now.
when it rains here it
rains like hell, remember?
oh, I'm gay now.
we live together, Doreen
and I. we have some
terrible arguments but
basically, I'm happy.
how are you?

the way things are

first they try to break you with grinding
poverty
then they try to break you with empty
fame.

if you will not be broken
by either
then there are natural methods
such as the usual diseases
followed by an unwelcome
death.

but most of us are broken long before
that
as it's meant to
be

by earthquake
flood
famine
rage
suicide
despair

or simply

by seriously
burning your nose
while lighting a
cigarette.

words for you

red dogs in green hell, what is this
divided thing I call
myself?

what message is this I'm offering
here?

it's so easy to slide into
poetic pretension.

almost all art is shot through with
poetic
pretension:

painting
sculpting
the stage
music

what is this foolish
strutting and posturing
we do?

why do we embroider everything we say
with special emphasis

when all we really need to do
is simply say what
needs to he said?

of course
the fact is

that there is very little that needs
to be said.

so we dress up our
little artful musings
and clamor for attention
so that we may appear to be
a bit more
important
or even more
truthful
than the others.

what is this I'm writing
here?

what is this you're
reading here?

is it no worse than the rest?

probably even a little bit
better?

strictly bullshit

now
there's a *new* one
going around:
he is whining and
telling people
that
I
was responsible
for him
not getting
published
by
The Black Vulture Press.

there have been
at least
three other poets
who have whined about
this.

well, luckily, I
don't have time to
read unsolicited manuscripts
or
advise
The Black Vulture Press.

but
if I did
I would have rejected
all three
along with
at least a dozen

other
dandies
who would like to
be published
there.

that's why I would
never
edit or publish
any
literary
gang.

at least
at the track
I can bet
on something
that won't whine and complain
and will show me
some fight
and
some run.

written before I got one

the best writers now
I'm told
have

word processors.

I'm not even sure what a
word processor
is.

but
no matter
the tree roots tangled
in my mother's bones

no matter
the shadows in the forgotten
canyon

no matter
the dream of the last
elephant

I'm not getting
one

whatever it
is

but
I hope it helps the best writers
get better

because I never could read them
anyhow.

and any boost for them
major or minor
will help us
all.

right?

straight on

there's nothing quite like driving the
hairpin curves on the Pasadena Freeway at 85
m.p.h.
hung over
checking the rearview mirror for officers of the
law
while peeling and eating tangerines that
sometimes
choke you with their
pulp, acid, seeds
as
your eyes fill with tears
your vision blurs
and you drive from memory
and on instinct
until
things get clear again.
finally you reach Santa Anita, that most beautiful race-
track,
and glide into the parking lot,
get
out, lock it, walk
in.

being 68 years old feels better than
30.
especially 30, that was the most depressing
birthday: you figured then that the gamble had been
lost.

what an awful
mistake you made then

38 years ago, about the time when they built
the
Pasadena Freeway.

remember this

believing what they say or write
is
dangerous
especially if they say or write
impossibly grand things
about
you

and you
are foolish enough to
believe them.

you are then apt to smash the
camera when somebody attempts to
photograph you in
public.

or you might get drunk
at your place
and shoot through the window
at your neighbor
with a
.44 magnum.

or you could purchase a very
expensive automobile
and then become irritated
with the less wealthy
in their old cars
who block your progress
on the
freeway.

or you might get married
too many times
or have too many
girlfriends.

or you could go to Europe
too often
or get high too
often.

you could
abuse
waiters.

refuse
autograph
seekers.

you could even
kill
somebody.

or
in a thousand
other ways
you could even finally
kill
yourself.

many
do.

now see here

playing with words as the mind fries and
pops like an egg left unattended in the
pan
while my cat crawls into a large paper bag
turns around
within and
looks out at me.

my woman is out tonight doing something
social.

I used to mind
I no longer mind.

if she can find pleasure
out there
I would say that
the world is better for
that.

the radio music is not very good
tonight
as I play with these words
as

I now
stare at
a red package of

50 white
envelopes.

what happened to those nights, man,
when you used to rip off poem after
poem?

oh shut up, I answer myself,
I don't feel at *all* like examining the
past, the present or the
future.

o.k., my brain says, I'm going on
strike too.

as my cat crawls out of the
paper bag
it's

a fairly slow night here.

little poem

little sun little moon little dog
and a little to eat and a little to love
and a little to live for

in a little room
filled with little
mice
who gnaw and dance and run while I sleep
waiting for a little death
in the middle of a little morning

in a little city
in a little state
my little mother dead
my little father dead
in a little cemetery somewhere.

I have only
a little time
to tell you this:

watch out for
little death when he comes running

but like all the billions of little deaths
it will finally mean nothing and everything:

all your little tears burning like the dove,
wasted.

part 4

real
loneliness
is not
necessarily
limited to
when
you are
alone.

Gertrude up the stairway, 1943

I think of Gertrude walking up that St. Louis
stairway
so many years ago
and myself just behind her
still almost a boy.
I think of Gertrude walking up that St. Louis
stairway
and never a stairway as taut with promise as
that one
with the landlady's pictures of Jesus
torn from cheap magazines
plastered here and there along the
walls.
I think of myself walking up that St. Louis
stairway
behind Gertrude
and into her room
going in there
the door closed firmly behind us
her pouring the claret
into tall thin glasses
in that dreary roominghouse
near that very large park
with its leafless trees of winter.
standing there
Gertrude seemed so lovely
so perfect
a girl beyond mere girlhood
a figure wrapped in a perfect
dream
and as
she stood there before me
she was finally

too perfect:
I downed my claret and begged my
leave
knowing that
following Gertrude up that St. Louis
stairway
was enough in
itself
it was
our one great moment together
and all that followed
would be
less
less
and I wanted to remember her like
that: perfect in the moment
before she wearied of the game and
we of each
other.

where was I?

I didn't know where I came
from or where I was
going.
I was lost.
I used to sit
in strange doorways
for hours,
not thinking
not moving
until I was asked
to move.

I don't mean that I was an
idiot or a
fool.
what I mean is that
I was
uninterested.

I didn't care if you intended
to kill me.
I wouldn't stop you.

I was living an existence that
meant nothing to
me.

I found places to stay.
small rented rooms. bars. jails.
sleep and indifference seemed
the only
possibilities.

all else seemed
nonsense.

once I sat all night long and looked
out at the Mississippi River.
I don't know why.
the river ran by and
all I remember is that it
stank.

I always seemed to be
on a cross-country
bus
traveling
somewhere.
looking out a dirty
window at
nothing at
all.

I always knew exactly how much
money I was
carrying.
for example:
a five and two ones
in my wallet
and a nickel, a dime and
two pennies in my right
front pocket.

I had no desire to speak
to anybody nor to be
spoken to.

I was looked upon as a
misfit and a
freak.
I ate very little food but
I was amazingly
strong.
once, working in a factory
the young boys, the bruisers,
were trying to lift a heavy
piece of machinery from the
floor.
they all failed.

"hey, Hank, try it!" they
laughed.

I walked over, lifted it,
put it down,
went back to
work.

I gained their respect
for some reason
but I didn't want
it.

at times I would pull down
the shades in my room
and stay in bed for a
week or more.

I was on a strange journey
but it was

meaningless.
I had no ideas.
I had no plan.
I slept.
I just slept
and I waited.

I wasn't lonely.
I experienced no self-pity.
I was just caught up in a
life in which
I could find no
meaning.

then I was
a young man a
thousand years old.

and now I am an old man
waiting to be born.

sloppy day

I had been up until 3 a.m. the night before.
heavy drinking: beer, vodka, wine
and there I was at the track
on a Sunday.
it was hot.
everybody was there.
the killers, the insane, the fools.
the disciples of Jesus Christ.
the lovers of Mickey Mouse.
there were 50,000 of them.
the track was giving away
free caps
and 45,000 of those people were
wearing caps
and there weren't enough seats
and the crappers were crowded
and during the races
the people screamed so loud
that you couldn't hear the
track announcer over the loudspeaker and
the lines were so long
it took you
20 minutes to lay a bet and
between running to the crapper
and trying to bet
it was a day you
would rather begin
all over again
someplace else
but it was too late now and
there were elbows and assholes every-
where and
all the women looked vicious and ugly and

all the men looked stupid and ugly
and suddenly
I got a vision of
the whole mass of them copulating
in the infield
like death fucking death,
stinking and stale;
they were walking all around
belching, farting
bumping into each other
gasping
losing
lost
hating the dream
for not coming
true.

then
some fat son of a bitch with
a pink pig's head perched
on his body
came rushing up to me
(why?)
and while
I pretended to be looking away
and as he closed in
I dug my elbow into his gut.
I felt it sink in like he was
a sack of dirty
laundry.

"mother," he gasped,
help . . ."

"you all right, buddy?" I
asked.

he looked as if
he was going to puke.
his mouth opened.
he cupped his hand
and a pair of
yellow-and-pink false teeth
fell into his palm.

I walked on through the crowd
and found a betting line.
I decided to bet the last 5 races
and leave.
the only way I would stay
would be for $900 an hour
tax free.

20 minutes later
I had made my bets
and I walked out to the parking lot
and to my car.
I got in
opened the window and
took off my shoes.

then I noticed
that I was blocked in.
some guy had parked behind me
in the exit aisle.

I started my engine

put it in reverse and
jammed my bumper against him.
he had his hand brake on
but luckily he was in neutral and
I slowly ground him back up against
another car.
now the other car wouldn't be able
to get out.

what made that son of a bitch
do that?
didn't he have any
consideration?

I put my shoes on
got out
and let the air out of his
left front tire.

no good.
he probably had a spare.
so I let the air out of his
left rear tire
got back into my car and
maneuvered it out of there
with great difficulty.

it felt good to
drive out of that racetrack.
it sure as hell felt better than
my first piece of ass and

most of the other pieces
which followed.

I got to the freeway and
turned the radio on and
the man told me
I had just won
the first of my 5 bets.
the horse paid $12.40.
at ten-win that was
$52 profit so
I wasn't on skid row
yet.

by the time
I got to my driveway
the man on the radio told me
that my next horse had
run out.
they had sent in a $75 long shot.
too bad.

I parked in the garage
climbed out
put my key in the front door
kicked it open
got my blade out: over 50%
of home burglaries occur during the
day.
I checked the immediate
visible area

walked into the bathroom
pulled back the shower curtain:
nothing.

I walked out
stood in the front room
and then I heard a sound
in the kitchen
and I yelled,
"O.K., FUCKER, COME ON OUT AND
WE'LL SEE WHO'S BEST!"

there was no answer.

"ALL RIGHT, FUCKER, I'M COMING
IN!"

I ran into the kitchen with my
blade extended.

my cat was sitting up on the
breadboard.
he looked at me, amazed, then leaped off
and zoomed out of the kitchen.

I walked into the bedroom and
switched on the tube.
the Rams and Lions were
playing.
I kicked my shoes off, stretched out
on the bed, said, "shit."
got up again, went downstairs,
cracked a beer, came up, let the

bathwater run and
stretched out on the bed again.

the QB took the ball
dropped back
looked downfield to pass and
didn't see the big lineman
breaking in
from his left.
the lineman blindsided the QB
like a trash collection truck.

the QB was making $2 million a year
and he earned much of it
on that play.

he didn't get up.
he couldn't.
he didn't want to.

I could have been a football
player
only my father, that son of a
bitch, said that a man went to
school to study,
not play.

I flipped off the tv
disrobed and
walked into the bathroom.
I turned off the water
tested it with my hand.

nothing like a hot bath
in a cold world.
I got in
stretched out,
the 230 pounds of me
pushing the water
through the emergency drain.

son of a bitch,
why did they build
5-foot bathtubs
in a world of
6-foot people?

nobody knew anything
and they certainly weren't getting
any smarter.

note on the telephone

often while I am up here
at the keyboard until 3 a.m.
or so
my wife gets on the telephone
downstairs
and conducts marathon
conversations
with her sister or her
niece
or somebody.
and as classical music
soothes my battered brain
and my fingers work
the keyboard
my wife works out
in her own way
on the telephone
discussing
for hours
whatever needs
to be
discussed.
some seem to need this
kind of intercourse.
their very souls
seem to be
nourished
by an endless wave
of
babble.

me, I'm just not a
telephone
person.

for me
it goes mostly
like this:
"sure. how are
you?
everything's
fine.
see you
later . . ."

I used to take
my telephone off
the hook
for days at
a time.
once I took
the damn
thing apart and stuffed the
bell and the
bell-ringer with
rags.
then I pissed on
it.

I believe
there's something
about the disembodied human
voice that

is not
reassuring.

you tell that to my wife
downstairs now and
she'll smile and say,
"have it your way!"

strange, isn't it?
how two such different people can
live under the same
roof

like
that.

at the edge

a smoky room at the edge, it's always
been a smoky room at the
edge.
the edge never goes away.
sometimes you understand it
better,
sometimes you even talk to it, you might
say, "hello, old friend,"
but it has no sense of humor, it slams you in the
gut, says,
"this is a serious business, I'm here to
kill you or drive you mad."
"all right," you reply, "I under-
stand."

tonight this room is smoky
and I am alone
listening to the silence.
I am tired of waiting on life,
it was so slow to arrive and so quick to
leave.
the streets and the cities are
empty,
love is on the damned cross
and death laughs in the back
room.

at the edge, the edge, the edge.

it's so sad: the flowers are still trying
to please me,
the sun shouts my name,
but my courage fails

as the animals look on with large
eyes.

this smoky room.
a stained rug.
a few books.
a painting or two.
a broken chair.
an empty pair of shoes.
a tired old man.

subordinated debt.

heads without faces,
seen in all the places

to go mad, to suicide or to
continue?

sitting here now is
ridiculously perfect: there's
nothing to compare it
with.

a palsied past and a short
future.

on days like this
one can be depressed by
the message in a fortune
cookie.

November creeps in on all fours
like a leper.

there still might be a place
for us
somewhere.

it's not the doing
it's the waiting.

it's not the waiting
it's the waste.

it's not the waste
it's the durability of
the waste.

one who thus believes,
concedes.

coming awake

yawning and stretching,
putting on a clean pair of underwear
and thinking,
you are not in jail and you don't have
cancer
but there are probably a few people out there
who would like to murder you but they
probably won't actually come and do
it.
you think about how
you once decided to be buried
near Hollywood Park
so you could hear the horses pound by
as you slept
but lately they've talked about
moving Hollywood Park elsewhere
because the neighborhood has gotten
so poor
so now you must live longer
until you learn where they plan to
relocate.
putting on your shirt and pants
you remember that
you are being taught in some
contemporary literature courses
and you fart as you walk down
the stairway.
strange thoughts are much like
hangovers: you feel better
without them.

then you wonder if there's any coffee left as
you open the front door and look out
to see if your car has been
stolen.

simple truth

you just don't know how to do it,
you know that,
and you can't do a lot of other
useful things either.
it's the fault of the
way you were raised,
some of it,
and you'll never learn now,
it's too late.
you just can't do certain things.
I could show you how to do them
but you still wouldn't do them
right.
I learned how to do a lot of necessary things
when I was a little girl
and I can still do them now.
I had good parents but
your parents never gave you enough
attention or love
so you never learned how to do
certain simple things.
I know it's not your fault but
I think you should be aware of how
limited you are.

here, let me do that!
now watch me!
see how easy it is!
take your time!
you have no patience!

now look at you!
you're mad, aren't you?

I can tell.
you think I can't tell?

I'm going downstairs now,
my favorite tv program is coming
on.

and don't be mad because
I tell you the simple truth about
yourself.

do you want anything from
downstairs?
a snack?
no?

are you sure?

and now

there are days
when it all goes
wrong.

on the freeway
at home
in the super-
market
and everywhere
else

continual
uninterrupted
ferocious
haphazard
assaults
on what
is left of
your
sanity and
sensibilities.

the gods first
play with you
and then
play
against
you.

your nerves
simmer until they're
raw.

no philosophical
shield
will protect you,
no amount of wisdom is
good enough.

you're hung out
as quarry
for the
dogs and
the
masses;
the breakdown
of the
machinery
and all
reason
is
total.

then
there's always
—suddenly—
a bright
smiling face
with dim
eyes, some
half-stranger
shouting
loudly:
*"hey, how ya
doing?"*

the face
all too close,
you see each
blemish and
pore in the
skin,
the loose
mouth is
like a broken
rotten
peach.

your only
thought
being,
shall I kill
him?

but then
you say,
"everything's
fine.
how about
you?"

and you
walk on past,
and the goat-
faced
half-stranger
is left
behind

as the sun
blazes down
through
acid
clouds.

you move
on
as the gods
laugh and
laugh
and
laugh,
you put one
foot
before the
other,
you swing your
arms
as the rusty
bell does
not ring,
as inside your
head
the blood
turns to
jello.

but
this day will end
this life will end
the vultures will

finally
fly
away.

please
hurry, hurry,
hurry.

crazy world

fellow mailed me a knife in the mail.
said it was a gift in appreciation of my
work.
the knife has a lever on the side,
slide it and the blade shoots
out and you're ready,
fast.
I doubt if I'll ever use this weapon
but it's nice to have a reader who is that
concerned for my
safety.
but really, I prefer readers who mail me
bottles of wine
even if some of them arrive
broken.
still, you should never drink anything
sent through the mails from an unknown
individual, somebody might try to poison
you.
but anything is preferable to the reader who
arrives in person at the door.
this truly upsets and angers me.
in this world, even minor fame can be a
major problem.

anyhow, I'm now using the knife the reader
sent me to clean my fingernails.

better this than ripping it deep into
somebody's guts.

I prefer to do that with the
poem.

good stuff

Red had a job cleaning rooming
houses
and he often brought me the
relics of the dead.
"nobody wanted his stuff. look
at this shirt. you can't buy a
shirt like this anymore.
and try on these glasses."

"thanks, Red."

"here, try on this robe. look at
that god-damned thing. ever seen
anything like it?"

"no, no, I haven't."

"he died Tuesday. try it on."

I tried it on.
it was thick like a bed quilt—
heavy, and yellow and green.
I tightened the belt.

"it's too big for you but
it looks good. he was a big
guy. I knew him well. he worked as a
janitor and drank malt beer."

"thanks, Red, I can use this."

"need any stockings? underwear?"

"no, I'm all right there."

Red left to go clean more
rooms.

·

that big robe was like something that
kings wore in the old days.
I really liked it, I'd never seen
anything like it in the stores.
it must have been passed down from generation
to generation.

my new girlfriend came over that
night and we sat around drinking.
I was still at the stage where I was
trying to impress her.
so after drinking a couple of beers
I told her, "I'll be right back."

I went into the bedroom and put on the
robe and then walked out with my drink
in my hand.

"Jesus Christ, what's that?"

"this, my dear, is class!"

"it's too big and it's
filthy! where did you get
it?"

"some guy died and they were going
to throw it away."

I sat down next to her.

"it stinks!"

"there's nothing wrong with death," I
told her, "there is nothing shameful
about death."

I decided not to show her the shirt.
or my new pair of reading
glasses.

we didn't make love that night.

•

the next time Red came by he had a pair
of leather gloves.
"this guy died last Friday. he worked in a
box factory. his relatives came by
and cleaned the place out. but they
forgot these. I found them on the closet
floor."

I put them on.
they were a little small but they were
like new, just a tiny hole in the tip of
one finger, left hand.

"thanks, Red, they're beautiful!"

"you can't get gloves like that any
more."

"yes," I told him, "don't I know
it?"

respite

fighting with women
playing the horses
drinking

sometimes I get too exhausted
to even feel bad

it's then that
listening to the radio
or reading a newspaper
is soothing,
comforting

the toilet looks kind
the bathtub looks kind
the faucets and the sink
look kind

I feel this way tonight

the sound of an airplane overhead
warms me
voices outside are
gentle and kind.

now I am content and
unashamed.

I watch my cigarette smoke
work up through the lamp shade
and all the people I have wronged
have forgiven me

but I know that I will go mad
again—
disgusted
frenzied
sick.

I need good nights like this
in between.
you need them too.

without them
no bridge would be
walkable.

the horse player

I've been watching them for decades.
the jocks change but the horses
look about the same.
the mutuel clerks change, the parking lot attendants change
but the tracks do not.
I have seen two riders killed, half a hundred horses break
down.
I have had horses pay over $300 and less than $2.80.
I've seen them run in downpours
and in fog so thick that the announcer couldn't make the call.
I've bet on thoroughbreds, quarter horses, harness nags,
even the dogs.
I've watched them in Mexico and America and in Europe.
I've met women at the track and I've left women at the track.
I've attempted to make a living at the track and if you want
stress, there it is.
once I spent 3 months living near the track at different motels,
     sitting
alone in the bars at night.
I've had a half dozen winning systems and a half dozen losing
ones but, at the time, I couldn't tell which was
which.
finally I quit
with my tail between my legs, got a job and played
the horses on the side.

I have wasted a lifetime at the racetrack
and to this moment, I still go every day.
I don't know any other place to go.
the toteboard flashes and I move in.
I have no idea what I am looking for or what I expect to
find.

I speak to nobody.
I sit with my latest system and wait for the next
race.

what else can I do?

displaced

burning in hell
this piece of me fits in nowhere
as other people find things
to do
with their time
places to go
with one another
things to say
to each other.

I am
burning in hell
some place north of Mexico.
flowers don't grow here.

I am not like
other people
other people are like
other people.

they are all alike:
joining
grouping
huddling
they are both
gleeful and content
and I am
burning in hell.

my heart is a thousand years old.

I am not like
other people.

I'd die on their picnic grounds
smothered by their flags
slugged by their songs
unloved by their soldiers
gored by their humor
murdered by their concern.

I am not like
other people.
I am
burning in hell.

the hell of
myself.

in search of a hero

as far as literature is concerned,
for a while, it was Hemingway, then I
noticed that his writing was imitating itself, he was
not really writing anymore.

as far as sex is concerned,
I began quite late and being fully rested
I gave it a roaring start, learning more from each woman
and applying it in all its fulsome aspects to the next, awakening
in strange bed after strange bed (and then back in some old
beds) looking out the window in the morning to check
on my car parked outside—and remembering that there was
another woman for later that day and maybe even another one that
night.
dinners, lunches, walks in the park,
walks by the sea, sometimes unexpectedly a brother,
a son, an ex-husband and, once, a current husband.
I knew of nobody with as many girlfriends as I had
who was drinking as hard at the same time.
I was penniless and stupid
and almost without reason.
I'd return now and then to my tiny dirty room
to find wild notes under
my door and in the mailbox from
anxious females.
I had no time to respond and some then became
enraged,
trashing my automobile, breaking into my
room, destroying everything in sight, female
hurricanes from hell.
and the phone rang without pause throughout
all this carnage, curses, wails, hang-ups, callbacks,

threats of love, threats of death, and if I took
the phone off the hook for a bit, soon the sound of
a racing motor, the screeching of brakes
and then a rock thrown through the window.
3 times there was an attempted murder
despite the fact that
I was old and ugly, worse than poor,
often without even toilet paper in
the bathroom. but somehow
in my demented state
I became my own hero.

I'd go into Black bars,
I'd go into biker bars,
I'd go drunk into Mexican bars,
I'd go anywhere,
I'd spit into the eye of God and
even into the face of the devil.
then I'd wake up somewhere
with someone new
in the morning
and the sun would be
shining
as if for me alone.

I bought the cheapest junk cars
off the lots
and drove them to Caliente, to
Mexico,
the woman saying,
"Jesus, you're driving this thing
like a maniac!"

I'd squander my meager dollars at the race
track
with bravado
as if all the gods were
on my side.

it all ended
some place, somewhere,
in a small
room in downtown L.A.
I was there with this beautiful
girl with long hair, so
young, such a fine body, such
long long hair, it was almost all
too much. I think it began
in a bar downstairs or around
the corner and it was
arranged that I was to have
sex with this child of
unbelievable beauty
but there
was also a large heavy Mexican
woman there, even
uglier than I and I turned to her
and said, "you can leave the
room now."

"I stay," she said. "I make sure
you not hurt her."

Christ, she was ugly.
the cheap flowers on
the wallpaper bloomed and

blossomed at me.
I wanted the obvious to be
obvious.

I looked at the ugly woman.
"I don't want her," I heard myself say,
"I want you."

"huh?"

"I'm going to fuck *you*!"

I rushed at her,
noticing at the same
time that the beautiful girl on
the bed was not moving, was not interested,
was not saying anything.

the big woman was
stronger than I,
she fought me off,
it was a
battle, I reached for her
breast,
I tried to kiss her
wretched
mouth
but she was full of
refried beans and
good
old-fashioned strength,
we banged against the
dresser,

spun around,
she shoved me away,
I crashed against the wall,
she rushed at me
and swung a heavy arm at
the end of which was attached
a metal claw I
had not noticed.
no hand, just this gleaming,
metallic, dangerous
claw.
I ducked under the claw
and she swung again.
I leaped aside and
ran to the door to find
it shut tight.
I ducked under the swinging
claw once more.
you have no idea how it
glinted, glinted in the
cheap light that
illuminated that heartless
room.
I flung open the door and
ran down the stairway
and she chased me down.
and I ran out into the street,
I ran and I ran
and when I looked around
she was gone.
and then luckily for me,
unlike so many other nights,
elsewhere and everywhere,

I remembered
exactly where I had parked
my car.

the albatross is a fake,
the universe is a shoe,
there are no heroes,
there is only a mouse
in the corner
blinking its eyes,
there is only a corner
with a blinking mouse,
two toads embrace
what's left of the sun
as the monkey
manages a tired
smile.

escapade

the end of grace, the end of what matters.
the eye at the bottom of the bottle
is ours
winking back.
old voices, old songs are a
snake which crawls
away.

men go mad looking into empty faces.
why not?
what else is there for them to do?
I have done it.

the eye at the bottom of the bottle
winks back.
it's all a trick.
everything is an illusion.
there must be something better somewhere.
but where?
not here.
not there.

slowly one crawls toward imbecility,
welcoming it like a lost
lover.

I weary of this contest with myself
but it's the only sport in
town.

burning, burning

a dismal god-damned night, the birds are limp
on the wire, the cats asleep on their backs,
legs stuck up into the lifeless
air. the homeless are still
homeless as a bell rings in my head
and
on the radio a man
shoves a Spanish rhapsody by Liszt
at me like an insult.
then, that's over and I'm told that eventually
something by Bach will be along if I manage to
stay awake.
as if to help, boat horns now blast from the
harbor.
if it weren't so hot tonight those things would all
fit together but instead
there's a madness in the air.

letter from a fellow from England today, he writes
that I am one of the few people he
admires.
well, he hasn't met me personally.

and, something else: there are no daring lives anymore,
none at all.
the only daring activity left is when
we kill.
and I'm not preaching or suggesting.
I'm simply telling you how
it is.

I get cranky in the heat, drink too much, smoke bits
of old cigars, pull at my left ear, scratch my

arms, think of bellybuttons, tombstones, cacti,
watchsprings, other oddities.

well, look, here's Bach and I'm still awake.
I need another reason to stay in this room full of ghosts,
some of them my own.
it could be worse, it will be.

nights like this. stuck here. grim reality
belches, more
boat horns blow.
the years hang strangled. I
burn my hand with a match.

the dream lies huddled, muddy.

confusion and sanctity reign.

effortless, painful, obnoxious, beautiful nights
like this. lives
like this.

there's too much to say, the dead
laugh as Bach enters
making palaces of sound, I can't stand it and yes
I can.

upon reading an interview with a best-selling novelist in our metropolitan daily newspaper

he talks like he writes
and he has a face like a dove, untouched by
externals.
a little shiver of horror runs through me as I read
about
his comfortable assured success.
"I am going to write an important novel next year," he says.
next year?
I skip some paragraphs
but the interview goes on for two and one-half pages
more.
it's like milk spilled on a tablecloth, it's as soothing as
talcum powder, it's the bones of an eaten fish, it's a damp
stain on a faded necktie, it's a gathering hum.
this man is very fortunate that he is not standing
in line at a soup kitchen.
this man has no concept of failure because he is
paid so well for it.
I am lying on the bed, reading.
I drop the paper to the floor.
then I hear a sound.
it is a small fly buzzing.
I watch it flying, circling the room in an irregular
pattern.

life at last.

nothing to it

"now," said the doctor, "I am going to explain the
entire procedure to you so you don't worry. we're
going to run a little tube down into your lungs. there's
a light on the end and we're going to look around.
also there is a little clipper attached and it will
take a snip here and there and bring some samples back so
we can have them analyzed.
the tubes are lubricated and slide right in. we enter
one nostril, go down through the throat and into the lung.
would you prefer we go in the left or the right
nostril?"

"the left," I said.

"the left? fine. now we want you on your back.
but first, maybe you'd like to look at the tubes?"

"no," I said.

"the whole procedure will be complete in from ten to
fifteen minutes. we're going to have a little look,
take a little snip, the tubes are lubricated, there's
nothing to it."

I glanced at the tubes. they looked like battery
cables.

"nurse," said the doctor.

"yes?" I said.

"no," said the doctor, "I was calling the
nurse."

"sorry," I said.

then I was on my back and two intent masked faces were bending
over me.

I had been on my way to the racetrack.
it was already past noon.
I was definitely going to miss the first
post.

this place

twenty-five thousand fools
lined up for a free hamburger
at the racetrack today and
got it.

in 1889
Vincent entered a
mental asylum in
St. Remy.

1564: Michelangelo, Vesalius,
Calvin die; Shakespeare, Marlowe,
Galileo
born.

caught a flounder yesterday,
cooked it
today.

midst the din of this
imperfect life
a blinding flash of
light
tonight:
when I let the
6 cats in
it was so
perfectly
beautiful
that
for a
moment
I

turned away
and faced the east
wall.

A.D. 701–762

these dark nights
I begin to feel like
the Chinese poet
Li Po:
drinking wine and writing
poems
writing poems and drinking
wine

all the while
aware of the strict limitations
that come with
being
human

then
accepting that

the wine and the poems
gently
intermixing:

yes, there is a peaceable place
to be found
in this unending
war
we call life

where
things
such as
light, shadow, sound
objects

become
gently
and meaningfully
fascinating.

Li Po
drunk on his
wine
knew very well that
just to know
one thing well
was
best.

regrets of a sort

I've written all these poems
just using the words
I know
even when my writing sometimes
became almost like
listening to your
neighbor
over the
backyard fence.

but I do like
the music of language:
the curl of the unexpected
word
the sensation
of a
tasty
almost never-used
near-virgin
word.

there are so many
of them.

at times
I read the dictionary
marveling
at the immensity of
that untouched
backlog.

there's a force
there

that properly exploited
would make
all I've written
seem
terribly simple.

yet
when I consider
the many poets
who have delved into this immense
backlog:

the educated
the cultured
the
all-knowing

it
doesn't appear to have
worked
very well
for them.
perhaps have they
chosen
the wrong
words?
for the wrong
reasons?

or without
taste?
or the need to
communicate?

whatever,
the users
of exotic words
have discouraged me
from trying to use my
vocabulary
as if it was
a shield
for pretenders.

and so
for the moment
for now
I am caught
with this
left with
this

and since you
have come with me
this
far

so
are you.

too young

I worked for a while in a picture frame
factory where my job was to hand-sand
the wood before it was assembled and
painted.

another man sat at a machine and he
ran the wood through and chopped it
into various lengths.
he worked the cutting blade by
stamping down on a lever with his
right foot.

I watched him for several days, then
I walked up to him.
"Jesus Christ, is that all you do?
I mean, just pump your foot up and
down for 8 hours?
doesn't that drive you
crazy?"

the man didn't reply and I went back
to my hand-sanding.

after that the other workers didn't
speak to me.

one week later the boss called me into
his office.
"we are going to have to let you
go."
he wrote out my check and I took it
and walked out of there.

outside as I walked along I felt
good, I felt that I understood something
very special.

about a month later
it was past midnight
and I was attempting to sleep
in a flophouse
alongside 35 or 40 men
on cots and
most of them were moaning
or snoring
loudly.

I still felt that I knew
something very special
which shows you
how little I really knew
at that particular
time.

listening to the radio at 1:35 a.m.

I switch the station:
a man plays the piano in grand
fashion.

somewhere else
there are nice homes
on the ocean shore
where you can
take your drink
out on the veranda
and
stand at ease and
watch the waves
listen to the waves
crashing in the dark
and yet
at the same time
you can feel crappy there
too

just like me now
having a dog fight
fighting for my life
within these 4 walls
20 miles inland.

unclassical symphony

the cat murdered
in the middle of the street

tire-crushed

now it is nothing

and neither are
we

as
we
look
away.

dinner for free

I was an unknown starving writer when I met this beautiful
lady who was young, educated, rich. I really can't
remember how it all came about. she had come by my destroyed
apartment a few times for brief visits. "I don't want sex,"
she told me. "I want you to understand that right from the start."
"o.k.," I said, "no sex."

one night she invited me to dinner (her treat). she
arrived in her new Porsche and we drove off.

the table was in front, it was a fancy place, and
there was a fellow with a violin and a fellow at the
piano.

I ordered wine and then we ordered dinner. it was quiet. too early
for the music, I guessed. it was good red wine.

the wine went quickly and I ordered another bottle.

"tell me about your writing," she said.

"no, no," I said.

the dinner arrived. I had ordered a porterhouse steak and fries.
she had something delicate. I don't remember what it was.
we began eating.

she started talking. it began easily enough. something
about an art exhibit. I nodded her on.

being an unknown starving writer it didn't take me very
long to clean my plate.

she began talking about the life of Mozart, slowly putting small morsels of food into her mouth.

I poured more red wine.

then she started talking about saving the American Indian from him/her self.

I quickly ordered another bottle of wine.

the waiter took our plates and she began pouring her own wine and tossing it down.

she told me that Immanuel Kant had a most brilliant mind, astonishingly brilliant.

as we sat her voice got louder and louder. she spoke more and more rapidly.

then the guy at the piano started playing and the guy with the violin joined in.

she raised her voice even more to be heard over the music.

she was back to saving the American Indian from him/her self.

I began getting a headache. as I sat and listened to her my headache got worse.

she began to explain what Jean Paul Sartre really meant.

the guy at the piano and the guy with the violin began to play louder
and louder to be heard over her.

finally I waved my arms at her and yelled, "LOOK, LET'S GO
    BACK TO MY
    PLACE!"

she paid the bill and I got her out of there. she talked all
the way back to my place. we parked and went in.

I had some scotch. I poured the scotch. I sat on the couch and
she sat on a chair across the room, talking loudly and
rapidly.

she was talking about Vivaldi, on and on about Vivaldi.

then she stopped to light a cigarette and I spoke.

"look," I told her, "I really don't want to fuck you."

she jumped up, knocked over her drink, began prancing around the
room. "oh, hahaha! I *know* you really want to fuck me!"

then she went into some type of energetic dance, holding her
cigarette over her head. she was very awkward, breathing
heavily and staring at me in a peculiar way.

"I have a headache," I told her. "I just want to go to bed and to
sleep."

"haha! you're trying to trick me into your bed!"

then she sat down and looked at me, still breathing heavily.

"I'm not going to let you fuck me!"

"please don't," I said.

"tell me about your writing," she said.

"look," I said, "will you please just get out of here and leave me alone?"

"ha!" she jumped up.

"ha! you men are all alike! all you think about is *fucking*!"

"I don't have the slightest desire to fuck you," I said.

"ha! you expect me to *believe* that?"

she grabbed her purse, ran to the door. then she was out the door, slamming it behind her.

and just like that, my beautiful, young, rich, educated lady was gone.

a song from the 70's

Hank, about the voices I hear, they talk to
me whenever I get in a medication jam like
I'm in now; I'm out of Valium and can't get any
until tomorrow.
I'm supposed to take Navane twice a day, one
at breakfast and one at bedtime plus three
Desyrel, one in the morning and two in the evening
plus 15 mg. of Valium a day, one tab usually around 9 in
the morning, one at 2 in the afternoon, one at 5 and one
before I go to sleep but I like to get high and usually
take 3 at a time.
I ran across a couple of old prescriptions for codeine and
Percodan last week and I took 40 codeines and 20
Percodans in 6 days. because I was
loaded I thought I threw the Percodan
prescription into the dumpster and scrounged
around in there for 30 minutes before I
discovered I had hidden it in my underwear so
my mother wouldn't find it.

I fell out of bed a few weeks ago and there was
this terrible black-and-blue mark on my leg near
my butt, so my mother made me go to the
Emergency Ward at Presbyterian Hospital and a young
intern there drew a circle around the mark with a
felt pen and gave me 30 tabs of Percodan and a
synthetic morphine shot, then I went to see my
internist and he looked at the black-and-blue mark
with the circle drawn around it and he wrote another
prescription for 40 more codeines.

I say legalize drugs for Christ's sake, and bring
back Country Joe and the Fish!

379

.188

it dissolves, it all dissolves: those we thought
were great, so exceptional—they dissolve;
even the cat
walking across the rug vanishes in a
puff of smoke;
nations break apart at the seams
and overnight become
tenth-rate powers;
the .330 hitter can no longer
see the ball, he dips to .188,
sits apart on the bench,
wonders about
the remainder of his life;
the heavyweight champ is knocked senseless by
a 40-to-one underdog;
it dissolves, it all dissolves—
lovers leave and
old cars break down
on the freeway at rush hour;
I look at a photo of myself
and think,
who's that
awkward
foolish
old man?
it dissolves—the nights of hurricane and
hunger
have turned
placid;
I search for a partial set of my teeth
on the bookcase
shelf;
and I can't even think of

a last line
for this poem;
sometimes
before his death
a man can see
his
ghost.

war some of the time

when you write a poem it
needn't be intense
it
can be nice and
easy
and you shouldn't necessarily
be
concerned only with things like anger or
love or need;
at any moment the
greatest accomplishment might be to simply
get
up and tap the handle
on that leaking toilet;
I've
done that twice now while typing
this
and now the toilet is
quiet.
to
solve simple problems: that's
the most
satisfying thing, it
gives you a chance and it
gives everything else a chance
too.

we were made to accomplish the easy
things
and made to live through the things that are
hard.

at last

I am sitting here
in darkest night
as one more poem
arrives
and says
wait,
wait,
watch me as I strut
across the page
letter by letter
like one of your
cats
walking across the
hood of your
car.
watch me,
here I
go
again
all the way to
Mexico
or Java
or down
into your
gut.
wait
some
more,
these nights
are meant for that,
and for
me
because

I control
you,
a captive there
sitting before
this
illuminated
screen.
you will do as I
want
because
I write
you,
not the other
way around.
I always have.
I always will.
I am the last
poem of this
night
and as you
sleep later in the
next room
in the dark
you will
forget about
me,
forget everything,
you with your
dumb mouth
open,
as you snore your
heavy
sleep,

I will be here
waiting,
immortal,
and
when you are
dead
and the black
sky flashes
red
for you
for the last time,
your dumb
bones
will amount to
nothing
more
than
dust.
but I will
live on.

misbegotten paradise

the bad days and the bad nights now come too
often,
the old dream of having a few easy
years before death—
that dream vanished as the other dreams
have.
too bad, too bad, too bad.
from the beginning, through the
middle years and up to the
end:
too bad, too bad, too bad.

there were moments,
sparkles of hope
but they quickly dissolved
back into the same old
formula:
the stink of reality.

even when luck was
there
and life danced in the
flesh,
we knew the stay
would be
short.

too bad, too bad, too bad.

we wanted more than
there could ever be:
women of love and
laughter,

nights wild enough for the
tiger,
we wanted days that
strolled through
life
with some grace,
a bit of
meaning,
a plausible use,
not something
just to
waste,
but something to
remember,
something
with which to
poke death
in the gut.

too bad, too bad, too bad.

in the totality of
all things, of course,
our petty agony is
stupid
and vain
but I feel that our
dreams were
not.

and we are not alone.
the relentless factors are
not a personal

vendetta against a
single
self.

others feel the same
searing
disorder,
go mad, suicide, go
dull, run stricken to
imaginary
gods,
or go drunk, go drugged,
go naturally
silly,
disappear into the mass of
nothingness
we call families,
cities,
countries.

but fate is not entirely
to blame.
we have wasted
our chances,
we have strangled
our own hearts.

too bad, too bad, too bad.

now we are the citizens of
nothing.

the sun
itself
knows
the sad truth of
how we surrendered
our lives
and deaths
to simple
ritual,
useless
craven
ritual,
and then
slinking away
from the face of
glory,
turning our dreams into
dung,
how we said
no, no, no, no,
to the most beautiful
YES
ever uttered:

life
itself.

my big night on the town

sitting on a 2nd-floor porch at 1:30 a.m.
while
looking out over the city.
it could be worse.

we needn't accomplish great things, we only
need to accomplish little things that make us feel
better or
not so bad.

of course, sometimes the fates will
not allow us to do
this.

then, we must outwit the fates.

we must be patient with the gods.
they like to have fun,
they like to play with us.
they like to test us.
they like to tell us that we are weak
and stupid, that we are
finished.

the gods need to be amused.
we are their toys.

as I sit on the porch a bird begins
to serenade me from a tree nearby in
the dark.

it is a mockingbird.
I am in love with mockingbirds.

I make bird sounds.
he waits.
then he makes them back.

he is so good that I laugh.

we are all so easily pleased,
all of us living things.

now a slight drizzle begins to
fall.
little chill drops fall on my
hot skin.

I am half asleep.
I sit in a folding chair with my
feet up on the railing
as the mockingbird begins
to repeat every bird song
he has heard that
day.

this is what we old guys do
for amusement
on Saturday
nights:
we laugh at the gods, we
settle old scores with
them,
we rejuvenate
as the lights of the city
blink below,

as the dark tree
holding the mockingbird
watches over us,
and as the world,
from here,
looks as good as it ever
will.

nobody but you

nobody can save you but
yourself.
you will be put again and again
into nearly impossible
situations.
they will attempt again and again
through subterfuge, guise and
force
to make you submit, quit and/or die quietly
inside.

nobody can save you but
yourself
and it will be easy enough to fail
so very easily
but don't, don't, don't.
just watch them.
listen to them.
do you want to be like *that*?
a faceless, mindless, heartless
being?
do you want to experience
death before death?

nobody can save you but
yourself
and you're worth saving.
it's a war not easily won
but if anything is worth winning then
this is it.

think about it.
think about saving your self.

your spiritual self.
your gut self.
your singing magical self and
your beautiful self.
save it.
don't join the dead-in-spirit.

maintain your self
with humor and grace
and finally
if necessary
wager your life as you struggle,
damn the odds, damn
the price.

only you can save your
self.

do it! do it!

then you'll know exactly what
I am talking about.

like a dolphin

dying has its rough edge.
no escaping now.
the warden has his eye on me.
his bad eye.
I'm doing hard time now.
in solitary.
locked down.
I'm not the first nor the last.
I'm just telling you how it is.
I sit in my own shadow now.
the face of the people grows dim.
the old songs still play.
hand to my chin, I dream of
nothing while my lost childhood
leaps like a dolphin
in the frozen sea.

CHARLES BUKOWSKI is one of America's best-known contemporary writers of poetry and prose, and, many would claim, its most influential and imitated poet. He was born in Andernach, Germany, to an American soldier father and a German mother in 1920, and brought to the United States at the age of three. He was raised in Los Angeles and lived there for fifty years. He published his first story in 1944 when he was twenty-four and began writing poetry at the age of thirty-five. He died in San Pedro, California, on March 9, 1994, at the age of seventy-three, shortly after completing his last novel, *Pulp* (1994).

During his lifetime he published more than forty-five books of poetry and prose, including the novels *Post Office* (1971), *Factotum* (1975), *Women* (1978), *Ham on Rye* (1982), and *Hollywood* (1989). Among his most recent books are the posthumous editions of *Betting on the Muse: Poems & Stories* (1996), *Reach for the Sun: Selected Letters 1978–1994, Volume 3* (1999), and *The Night Torn Mad with Footsteps: New Poems* (2001).

All of his books have now been published in translation in over a dozen languages, and his worldwide popularity remains undiminished. In the years to come, Ecco will publish additional volumes of previously uncollected poetry and letters.